# FREE AS A BIRD

Stevie wandered out onto the balcony to look through the huge window at Central Park. *There's freedom out there*, she thought.

If only she were on the other side of the glass. If only she were outdoors.

Stevie looked at her watch. She had a whole two hours. She looked at the park. It wouldn't hurt to take a break from all this culture. In fact, she owed it to herself. A breath of fresh air was all she needed.

She walked through the Egyptian exhibit back to the main hall. To the right was the museum gift shop. Stevie could buy postcards later.

She wiggled through the knot of tourists and hurried down the stairs. She ran along an endless fountain and turned left. Suddenly she was in the park.

*Fresh air. Freedom.*

# THE SADDLE CLUB

# PAINTED HORSE

## BONNIE BRYANT

A SKYLARK BOOK

NEW YORK · TORONTO · LONDON · SYDNEY · AUCKLAND

RL 5, 009–012

PAINTED HORSE

A Bantam Skylark Book / March 1998

ISBN 0-553-48625-X

Published simultaneously in the United States and Canada.

PRINTED IN THE UNITED STATES OF AMERICA
OPM      0  9  8  7  6  5  4  3

*I would like to express my special thanks
to Helen Geraghty for her help
in the writing of this book.*

**1**

"I BET STEVIE'S having lunch at one of those posh restaurants where models eat," Lisa said.

"But models never eat," Carole said.

"So they're watching Stevie eat," Lisa said with a laugh. Their best friend, Stevie Lake, was famous for her large appetite and for eating weird combinations of food, like blueberry sherbet with butterscotch sauce and chocolate-mint chips.

Stevie, Lisa Atwood, and Carole Hanson were members of The Saddle Club. The club had only two rules: Members had to be totally horse-crazy, and they had to help each other out whenever possible.

The three friends would have been doing something

together, but Stevie had gone to New York City on a class trip. Normally, she never would have done anything school-related over a vacation, but this trip was giving her the opportunity to bring her grades up. And, Lisa and Carole knew, if Stevie's grades slipped too far, she'd lose her riding privileges. Besides, going to New York sounded like fun.

"She's probably eating a buffalo steak," Carole said.

"Or hearing the latest gossip from Skye," Lisa said. Skye Ransom was a well-known actor whom The Saddle Club had met when they had all been in New York together. His horse had run away, and The Saddle Club had helped him catch it. He and the girls had been fast friends ever since.

When Skye had written The Saddle Club saying he was going to be starring in a Broadway show, Stevie had written back telling him a group from her class was going to be in New York at the same time. Skye had promised to introduce Stevie to the true glamour of the Big Apple.

Lisa and Carole, on the other hand, were stuck in Willow Creek on a miserable rainy Wednesday. It was their vacation, just as it was Stevie's, and they had been planning to ride all week. They couldn't ride outdoors because of the rain, and the indoor ring was booked for classes and private lessons, so they were sitting in a stall at Pine Hollow trying to figure out what to do.

"If I were there, I could help Stevie eat gourmet food," Carole said.

"I could help her ride in limousines," said Lisa.

"She really needs us," Carole said. "Maybe we could talk our parents into sending us up to New York."

"What's this?" came a voice. "Who's going to New York?"

They looked up and saw Max Regnery, the owner of Pine Hollow Stables, staring down at them. His blue eyes were stern. "Who wants to go to New York when there's so much to do here?"

"If we were ducks, there would be plenty to do," Lisa said.

"I guess you've forgotten that this Saturday is the Spring Tune-Up," Max said. The Spring Tune-Up wasn't a competition. After the winter, riders and horses weren't ready for a full-scale horse show. The Tune-Up was a way of celebrating the end of snow and ice.

"I guess there's a lot to be polished," said Carole glumly as she got to her feet. Usually Carole loved anything to do with horses—even cleaning tack. But the thought of Stevie in New York hobnobbing with stars and eating gourmet meals made polishing leather seem dull.

"The tack has to be sparkling by Saturday," Max said.

Carole and Lisa looked at each other. Were they supposed to clean gear all week? This was vacation!

As they followed Max to the tack room, horses pawed and snorted, sending out a smell that was halfway between a wet blanket and a soggy dog.

"Phew," Lisa said.

Max's blue eyes twinkled. "You're right," he said to Lisa. "The horses and ponies do smell bad. After you finish with the tack, you can start grooming them."

Lisa knew how much work was involved in grooming a horse on a rainy day. Their coats were sticky, so dirt and dander wouldn't come out and their manes got tangled.

"It's not only humans who have bad hair days," Carole said. "Horses do, too."

"That means that Starlight and Prancer need you even more than usual," said Max, referring to their horses. "And while you're at it, make sure that Belle is groomed, too." Belle was Stevie's horse.

"Me and my big mouth," Carole muttered.

As they walked into the tack room, Lisa noticed that there were very few other riders around. Only total horse nuts would come to the stable on a day like this.

"Don't forget to use metal polish on the bridles," Max said.

4

"Of course not," said Carole.

"And don't forget to clean the undersides of everything," Max added.

"Don't worry," Lisa said. As if she and Carole would try to cut corners!

Lisa looked around the tack room at the saddles—there were about a million—and the bridles—there were a trillion—and the halters—there were a zillion. She realized that she and Carole would be there all that day and all the next. "Where should we start?" she asked Carole.

Carole ran a hand through her wavy black hair. "Let's start with the halters," she said.

"The halters!" Lisa said. They were the least satisfying to polish. A lot of them were old, and they were made with leather that was strong rather than beautiful. No matter how much you polished a halter, it usually looked homely.

Lisa knew that Carole wanted them to do the most boring jobs first. *Carole is so disciplined,* she thought. *She always does the right thing—at least when it comes to horses.* For a second Lisa missed Stevie horribly. If Stevie had been there, she'd have turned the whole thing into a game. They'd be laughing and throwing sponges. They'd have a good time *and* get the tack clean.

"Why not?" Lisa said, letting the heels of her boots thud on the floor as she crossed the room. She gathered a load of halters and dumped them in a messy pile in the center of the floor. "This will only take a couple of years."

Carole got a bucket of water and a carrier with sponges, rags, saddle soap, and metal polish. "It won't be so bad," she said. "The leather is dry, but the glycerin in the saddle soap will soften it. Wait and see—it'll be like magic."

"Yeah, right," Lisa said.

"I'll do the metal. You do the leather," Carole said.

Doing the metal was the worst part because metal polish smelled bad and took a lot of rubbing. Lisa knew that Carole was trying to be nice. She picked up a halter with straps so old and dry that they were twisted. "They should throw this thing away," she said.

"That's a great halter," said Carole.

*Carole never met a piece of tack she didn't like,* thought Lisa.

But fifteen minutes later the halter did look great. The saddle soap had softened the leather and made it supple. The metal polish made the buckles and rings shine.

"You were right. Underneath the grime, it was a thing of beauty," said Lisa.

There was a rich, warm smell in the air. It was a little like the smell of gardenias, but more delicate, and a little like the smell of lilacs, but richer. Lisa looked up to see Veronica diAngelo. Her black hair was combed into a perfect pageboy, and her skin looked even creamier than usual. She was wearing a camel hair riding jacket and a pair of custom-made tan breeches, and her boots were gleaming. As far as Lisa knew, Veronica never came out in the rain. Lisa wondered what was up.

"Hello, fashion misfits," said Veronica.

Lisa felt her hand rise to her hair, which was fuzzy from the dampness. She looked down at her jeans, which were streaked with bits of hay.

"You look even worse than usual," said Veronica.

"It's raining, Veronica," Lisa said. "What are you doing out in this weather?"

"My public wants me," said Veronica, smoothing her hair. "How can I say no?"

Lisa looked around, but there was still no one else there. "Excuse me? Maybe your public forgot to come."

"They're on their way," Veronica said grandly. "Listen."

Lisa listened, but all she could hear was the splattering of the rain.

"Darlings," said Veronica. "Today I become famous."

STEVIE WAS IN trouble. She couldn't decide whether to wear the sunglasses with the black frames or the ones with the gold frames. She wanted to look totally sophisticated. She did not want to look like some out-of-town hick. She tried the glasses with black frames and checked her reflection in the window of the van. She looked mysterious . . . maybe a little dangerous. Then she tried on the ones with gold frames. She looked dramatic . . . practically dazzling. She decided to go with the gold. "Get ready, New York," she muttered.

Stevie sat back and sighed. This trip would have been perfect if Lisa and Carole had been with her. But since they didn't go to Stevie's school, Fenton Hall, there was no way they could have come. Stevie would have to have fun for all three of them.

Veronica diAngelo went to Fenton Hall, but she had snootily refused to go on the trip. She'd said that New York bored her to tears. Stevie figured that when she got back with tales of hanging out backstage at a Broadway show, Veronica would die of jealousy. Just to make sure that this happened, Stevie had brought along a camera to document every exciting moment of her visit.

Stevie fished her camera out of her backpack and passed it to Helen, the girl sitting next to her. "Snap me in these," she said, adjusting her sunglasses.

"Same old Stevie," said Helen as she took Stevie's picture.

The van rolled to the top of a hill. On the other side of the river, Manhattan sparkled in pure silver light. Stevie sighed. She could feel an adventure coming on.

The van went down into the Lincoln Tunnel. The

yellow tiled walls seemed to go on forever. When the van came up, it was in the middle of Manhattan.

"Bright lights, here I come," said Stevie.

The trip leader, Mrs. Martin, stood up at the front of the van and clapped for quiet. Usually Mrs. Martin was overserious, in Stevie's opinion. But today she was wearing a black dress with a red scarf draped around her shoulders and looked practically snappy. Stevie smiled, thinking that New York had a good effect on everyone.

"As we explore this morning, I want you to look with your hearts and not your heads," Mrs. Martin said.

"I can do that," Stevie mumbled to herself.

"I want you to find something that you really care about," Mrs. Martin said.

"That will not be a problem," said Stevie, sitting back and thinking of how she was going to go backstage with Skye and meet New York's most glittering people.

"Be sure to keep notes," Mrs. Martin said. "You think you'll remember everything, but you won't."

"Like I would forget," said Stevie.

The van traveled up a street crowded with sidewalk cafés. People were sitting outside enjoying the first warm spring sun. As they slowly rode past a bakery, Stevie saw trays of tiny tarts with raspberries and whipped cream, apples and raisins, and peaches and strawberries. "I could go for a snack," she said.

But the van kept moving. A block later it was in Central Park. The grass was just beginning to turn green. There were in-line skaters and joggers. Stevie smiled. In New York, everyone had fun.

The van turned left and entered an underground garage. Stevie let out a whoop of joy.

Helen turned and gave her a funny look. Stevie figured she must be nervous about being in New York. After all, it took nerve and style to cope with the city.

Mrs. Martin explained that their bags would be delivered to the hotel. All the group had to do was follow her. They walked down a sidewalk to a brightly lit doorway. Mrs. Martin turned to the class and smiled. "Welcome to the most fascinating spot on earth."

"I'm ready," Stevie said.

But then she noticed that there was formal lettering on the doorway, and a man in a gray uniform was standing inside the door. As Stevie walked closer, she realized that if she took off her sunglasses, it would be easier to read the lettering. It said *Metropolitan Museum of Art*.

Stevie's heart sank.

"You're going to love this, Stevie," Ms. Dodge, the assistant teacher, said.

"Yeah, right," Stevie muttered.

"What's that, Stevie?" Ms. Dodge asked with a smile.

"Uh, my shoes are too tight," said Stevie, leaning down and loosening her laces.

"We'll be visiting two or three museums a day," Ms. Dodge said. "Aren't you thrilled?"

*Chilled would be more like it*, Stevie thought. Bitterly, she remembered that Veronica diAngelo had refused to go on the trip. Veronica must have known. Her father was on the board of trustees of Fenton Hall. He must have heard that the trip was one big museum visit and told Veronica.

At this moment, Veronica was probably lazing in bed. Or riding her horse, Danny, at Pine Hollow. Stevie groaned.

"What's that, Stevie?" asked Ms. Dodge.

"I guess I'm overwhelmed with excitement," Stevie said.

"Just wait until you see the museum's treasures," Ms. Dodge said.

Mrs. Martin led them upstairs to a huge marble lobby and then through the Egyptian wing. Mummies weren't so bad, Stevie thought. She could handle a mummy or two. But Mrs. Martin walked through the Egyptian gallery without looking right or left. She led the class through a glass door into a place with high windows, a lot of plants, and antiques.

Stevie didn't like antiques. She had an aunt who had

a house full of them. The place was like one big booby trap. When you sat on something, it groaned and creaked and threatened to collapse. And if it collapsed, that would be thousands of dollars down the drain.

Mrs. Martin gathered the class. "I know you're as excited to be here as I am," she said.

"Totally," Stevie muttered. She felt an arm go around her, and Ms. Dodge was smiling at her. She figured the smile was a warning and that she had better stop complaining.

"I want each of you to pick an object," Mrs. Martin said. "It should be from around the turn of the century, the late 1800s or the early 1900s. It should be something that has special meaning for you. When you return home, you'll be asked to write an eight-page paper on it." A groan went up from the class. "That includes illustrations. You can buy as many postcards as you want." There was a collective sigh of relief. "But there must be at least four pages of text," Mrs. Martin continued. Another groan. "You'll have no trouble filling them," she said. "During our trip we will visit many museums and other points of interest to help you understand your chosen object."

*Points of interest, ha!* thought Stevie. *Points of boredom would be more like it.*

## 2

"YOU'RE GOING TO BE famous?" Lisa asked Veronica. "Famous for what?"

Veronica twirled a lock of glossy black hair around her finger. "Station WCTV is planning a special feature on talented young people. It's called 'Genius Kids.' "

"Oh," Lisa said. From the glow in Veronica's eyes, she could tell that the other girl was telling the truth. "Can I ask you a question?"

"But of course," said Veronica.

"What are you a genius at?" said Lisa.

Veronica's dark eyes flashed, and she put her fists on her hips. Her bright red lips came together in an angry line. "Riding, of course."

Lisa and Carole exchanged startled looks. Veronica was a pretty good rider—though she wasn't good at taking care of her horse and her tack—but she wasn't exactly a genius.

"Who decided you were a genius?" Lisa asked. The question went unanswered.

Wheels splashed in the mud outside. Carole stepped over to the window of the tack room. A white-and-blue WCTV truck was pulling up.

When it stopped, Melody Manners, a star reporter at the station, climbed out of the passenger side. She had fine blond hair and dazzling blue eyes.

Melody held a raincoat above her head and ran toward the stable. Lisa noticed that the reporter was wearing a pink jacket and a pale green blouse. Below the waist, though, she was wearing blue jeans and a pair of sensible brown boots. Following her was a cameraman.

Melody looked at the three girls. "Now, which of you is Veronica?"

Veronica stepped forward with a smile. "That's me."

Melody took in Veronica's fancy boots and breeches and perfect hair. "I should have known," she said. "Mr. Wall said you'd be fantastic."

"Who?" said Veronica.

"The head of the station," said Melody. "He gave us your name."

Veronica's smile faded, and her eyes narrowed. Color rose to her cheeks. Lisa and Carole looked at each other. Veronica's father knew everyone who was rich and powerful in Willow Creek. He must have talked a friend into naming Veronica a Genius Kid.

Lisa realized that Veronica thought she had been named a Genius Kid on her own, without her father's help. Lisa suddenly felt sorry for Veronica.

"You'll be great," Lisa said.

"Of course I will," said Veronica, glaring at Lisa.

Carole stepped forward. "Listen, you're representing Pine Hollow Stables, and that's what's important."

"Good thinking," came Max's deep voice from behind Carole. "All our riders represent us, and I know that Veronica will do a fine job."

"She's a good rider," Lisa said.

Anyone else would have been grateful for the compliment, but Veronica bit her lip and looked from Lisa to Carole with fury.

"So what's on the program?" Melody asked Max. "What would you guys be doing if I weren't here?"

Max grinned. "Do you want to know the truth?"

"Absolutely," said Melody. "I want this show to be true to life."

"On a rainy day like today, we'd be polishing tack," Max said.

"Then we'll do that," said Melody.

Veronica looked scared. Her usual method of cleaning tack was to get someone else to do it.

Melody motioned for the cameraman to start shooting. "We're at Pine Hollow Stables with Genius Kid Veronica diAngelo. Being a Genius Kid isn't all ribbons and applause. A lot of it is plain hard work. Today, Veronica is going to clean tack."

Veronica looked around desperately. Then she caught sight of the halter that Lisa and Carole had just cleaned. She leaned down and picked it up, and then she picked up a stiff, muddy halter.

"This is before," said Veronica, holding up the dirty halter. "This is after," she said, holding up the polished one.

"That's some difference," said Melody, peering at the two halters. "You did a great job, Veronica."

"Thanks," Veronica said with a smug smile.

"Show us how it's done," said Melody.

Fear flickered in Veronica's eyes.

No way was Lisa going to let Pine Hollow look bad. "I'll get your saddle," she said to Veronica. Veronica gave her a suspicious look.

Carole gave Lisa a quick nod. "And I'll get the saddle soap and the sponges," she said.

As Lisa and Carole headed off, Max threw them a grateful look.

16

Lisa picked up Veronica's saddle. It was a tawny dressage saddle with a deep seat and long flaps. It was light and perfectly balanced. *A saddle like this should belong to a great rider like Carole,* Lisa thought. But, in a way, that didn't matter. This saddle deserved good care, no matter who owned it. She put the saddle on a wooden saddle horse.

Carole came over with a bucket of water and a carrier filled with tins of polish, saddle soap, and sponges. She held them out to Veronica.

Veronica knew enough to know that soaping a saddle was not a simple matter. If she did it the wrong way, there were bound to be TV viewers who would notice and complain.

Carole didn't want to let Max down, so she said, "Why don't I clean it while you explain what I'm doing, Veronica?"

Veronica looked relieved. She turned to the camera and smiled. "Cleaning a saddle isn't as easy as you might think."

Carole took off the girth, the stirrup leathers, and irons. "I'm stripping the saddle," she whispered.

"Carole is stripping the saddle," Veronica said.

Holding the saddle by the pommel, Carole held it over the bucket of water and washed the inside with a sponge. When she was done, she dried it with a chamois cloth. And then she got a dry sponge, opened the tin of

17

saddle soap, put a dab on the sponge, and applied it with a circular motion.

"You need a dry sponge and a wet sponge," Carole whispered.

"Notice that she uses two sponges," said Veronica. "One wet. The other dry."

Lisa sneaked a glance at Max. He was looking relieved. It wasn't his fault that Veronica had been picked as a Genius Kid. He would have picked Carole if he'd had a choice.

Carole put the saddle back on the saddle horse. She washed the seat, the flaps, and the leather underneath the flaps with the wet sponge. She struggled to get rid of a greasy black mark. "It's called a jockey," she whispered.

"Those marks are called jockeys," Veronica said. "They must be removed."

Lisa sighed with relief. The demonstration was going well. Veronica looked good, Carole looked good, and Pine Hollow looked good.

Carole dried the wet leather with a chamois cloth. "If it's not dry, there'll be lather," she whispered. "When it dries, lather collects dust."

"Make sure the leather is dry before you put on the soap," Veronica said. "Otherwise the soap will lather. And the lather will dry and accumulate dirt."

"Great," Melody said. "But now we want to see you do something, Veronica. Why don't you provide the finishing touches?"

Veronica picked up a dry sponge and a tin. The only problem was that she hadn't picked up the tin of saddle soap. She had picked up a tin of black leather polish.

"Er," Lisa said. "Wait—"

"I think I know what I'm doing," Veronica snapped.

"Please," whispered Carole, looking at the black polish with an expression of misery.

Veronica threw Lisa and Carole a scornful look. She lifted the lid of the tin and put her sponge in the black polish.

"Excuse me," Carole said, reaching for the polish.

Veronica rolled her eyes and put a bold black streak across the saddle.

STEVIE WAS IN big trouble. She knew she had to choose a special object for her paper—she really needed this grade. And she knew Ms. Dodge was keeping an eye on her. But she couldn't make up her mind. Everything looked equally boring.

There was something called a highboy, which was actually just a large chest of drawers. Stevie couldn't understand why something so boring had such an interesting name. And then there was a triangular chair.

Ten minutes sitting in that chair and you'd feel like a pretzel. And then there was a footstool covered with shiny black fabric.

"Isn't that nice?" said Ms. Dodge with a sigh.

"I guess," said Stevie.

"Do you know what it's covered with?" said Ms. Dodge.

"No," said Stevie.

"You'll be interested, Stevie, because I know you love horses," she said.

Stevie wondered what a footstool had to do with horses.

"That shiny black fabric is horsehair," Ms. Dodge said.

Stevie jumped back. What a way for a noble horse's mane and tail to end up—on a footstool.

Ms. Dodge couldn't seem to tear herself away from that footstool. Stevie wandered out onto the balcony to look through the huge glass window at Central Park. She saw a squirrel scramble up a tree and scoop a nut out of a hole. A pair of blackbirds sat on the back of a bench, cawing at each other. One rose; then the other rose. They swept up into the sky. *There's freedom out there*, Stevie thought.

"You've got to see this fire screen," Mrs. Martin called to Ms. Dodge. Ms. Dodge hurried off to look.

There were people who thought fire screens were exciting, Stevie realized. That was okay. It was a free country.

Stevie turned back to the window. Sometimes there were horses in Central Park. She knew this because she had ridden there on the previous visit when she and Lisa and Carole had met Skye Ransom.

If only she were on the other side of the glass. If only she were outdoors.

"Now, Stevie." Stevie jumped guiltily. It was Ms. Dodge. "It's time to select your object," she said. "We'll meet in the main hall near the museum store at four." She smiled. "Don't forget to get a postcard of your object."

"No problem, Ms. Dodge," said Stevie.

As soon as Ms. Dodge moved away, Stevie looked at her watch. She had a whole two hours. She looked at the park. It wouldn't hurt to take a break from all this culture. In fact, she owed it to herself. A breath of fresh air was all she needed.

She walked through the Egyptian exhibit back to the main hall. To the right was the museum gift shop. Stevie could buy postcards later.

She wiggled through the knot of tourists and hurried down the stairs. She ran along an endless fountain and turned left. Suddenly she was in the park.

*Fresh air. Freedom.* She raised her arms and a bird burst up out of a bush.

21

"Way to go," she said to the bird. "Don't let anybody keep you down."

She climbed a sloping sidewalk until she was on a hill behind the museum. The road was filled with joggers, skaters, cyclists, and kids on tricycles.

Stevie felt excitement rise inside her. It was like the beginning of a cross-country event or the beginning of a hunt. If she'd been on Belle, she'd have leaned forward and said, "Go, girl."

She was alone now, so she said it to herself. "Go, Stevie."

Next thing she knew, she was part of the stream of cyclists and skaters and runners. She was on the move.

VERONICA GASPED AT the black streak. Lisa gulped. This was really going to make Pine Hollow look bad. Their supposedly best rider didn't know the difference between saddle soap and leather polish.

"Somebody got the lids reversed," Carole said. "Veronica thought she was picking up saddle soap when she was picking up black polish." The truth was that Veronica hadn't bothered to check that she was taking the right tin, but Carole was trying to make the stable look good.

Veronica rolled her eyes significantly. She was clearly implying that Carole had gotten the caps mixed up.

Lisa was furious. No one was going to do that to Carole. "It's me," she said. "I'm so absentminded. I just do these things. I don't know why."

Carole couldn't believe her ears. Lisa was the least absentminded person she knew. But she knew that Lisa was only trying to protect the honor of Pine Hollow. "It was both of us," Carole said quickly. She picked up a clean sponge and loaded it with saddle soap. Their only hope was to get the black polish off the saddle before it sank into the leather.

Lisa picked up another sponge, loaded it with more saddle soap, and started scrubbing, too.

Veronica crossed her arms and watched as Lisa and Carole struggled to remove the polish.

Lisa's and Carole's heads bumped as they scrubbed. This might be Veronica's saddle, but it was a beautiful one. They wanted to make it like new again.

"Ohhh," Lisa groaned as she scrubbed at a particularly tough spot. Finally it came away. She stood back. There was no trace of black polish.

Lisa and Carole looked at each other and sighed with relief.

"Thank goodness," said Melody. "I really thought that saddle was ruined."

"Yes," Veronica said. "It was a close call. It shows what carelessness can do."

Lisa nodded solemnly.

"I'd like to commend Lisa and Carole," Veronica continued in a sugary voice. "This shows that even if people make errors, they can fix them."

The cameraman turned the camera to Lisa and Carole, who grinned bravely.

Meanwhile, Lisa was thinking that all her friends watched WCTV. They'd want to know how she could make such a silly error. From now on her life was going to be miserable. She looked over at Carole. She could tell that Carole was embarrassed, too.

"So what's on for tomorrow?" said Melody, turning to Max.

Max thought for a second. "To tell you the truth, we'll be cleaning bridles."

Veronica's eyes widened, but then she caught herself and smiled. "It's one of my favorite things," she said. "I love cleaning bridles."

Lisa and Carole gave each other despairing looks. Tomorrow they would have to be even more helpful.

A HORSE-DRAWN CARRIAGE rumbled past Stevie as she walked through Central Park. The carriage had white wheels and red seats, and the driver was wearing a top hat and a black coat with tails. The horse looked kind of bored, but it was a real horse.

Stevie followed the flow of skaters and joggers along a curving road. Eventually she came to a sign that said BOAT HOUSE in front of a cheerful redbrick building on the edge of a lagoon. At tables along the water, people were eating and talking. Stevie smelled the enticing odor of french fries. *Fries would taste good right now*, she thought. *With ketchup.* But she didn't stop. It felt too good to be moving. She just wanted to walk outside.

As Stevie walked past the lagoon, she saw people in rowboats. Other people were in a gondola propelled by a man standing up and handling a pole. She had never seen anything like it. But she didn't stop to investigate. She wanted to see as much of the park as possible.

The road turned right, and after a while she heard cheerful, tinny music. There was something familiar about it. She followed a path down the hill and saw a carousel with colorful wooden horses. She sighed. The horses in the carousel were beautiful.

Stevie had to smile. There was a line of small kids with their parents. Stevie remembered that when she was little, riding the carousel in the Willow Creek mall had been the scariest and most exciting experience of her life. Stevie got in line, even though she felt a little silly because she was a lot younger than the parents and a lot older than the kids.

When she got to the head of the line, the ticket seller, who was a chubby man with fuzzy hair, said, "How many?"

"Just one," Stevie said. "There's only me."

"You can ride more than once," the man said with a smile.

When Stevie was little, she never got to ride the carousel for as long as she wanted. Now she could ride forever.

"Give me five," she said. "No, ten."

The man smiled more broadly and counted out the tickets.

When the carousel stopped, half the kids didn't get off. There were only two horses left when it was Stevie's turn to get on. She chose a black one and climbed on. She grinned happily. New York was starting to be a lot more fun.

"Excuse me," said a man with a baseball hat on backward. "Please strap yourself in."

"Me?" said Stevie. "I know how to ride."

"It's the rules," the man said, smiling at her.

Stevie put the leather strap around her waist and buckled it. She remembered how safe the strap had made her feel when she was little. A bell rang, and the carousel lurched into motion. She thought about how when she was little the carousel had seemed as fast as the wind.

There was a squeal of fear from a little kid in front of her. "I'm here," his mother said, putting her arms around him.

Stevie's horse moved up. She imagined she was rising over the treetops. The horse went down. It was like sinking into the earth. Up and down. Stevie put a hand on the horse's neck. "You've got nice gaits," she said. "Very regular and smooth. If you weren't wood, we could ride off into the sunset together."

"You can't do that," said the man with the baseball hat. He had climbed on the moving carousel and was taking tickets. "The carousel has been here since the turn of the century. This horse is about ninety years old."

"He looks pretty good for a ninety-year-old horse," Stevie said.

"He's one of my favorites," the man said with a smile. He walked forward to take more tickets.

"I like you," Stevie said to the horse. "I'm going to give you a name. I think I'll call you Ralph." When the carousel stopped moving, Stevie whipped her camera out of her backpack and took a photograph of Ralph.

Stevie rode and rode until it seemed as if Central Park were moving and she and Ralph were standing still. Finally her tickets ran out. She climbed off the carousel and wobbled. She had been going around so long that she'd lost her sense of balance. In fact, she felt kind of strange.

Standing on the grass was a mare with a rich brown

coat and large, intelligent eyes. The mare had long white socks on the right side and short white socks on the left. She looked almost like Belle, Stevie's horse.

*I'm going crazy*, Stevie thought. *I miss Belle so much I imagine that she's here.* She looked up and saw, to her relief, that the mare was real. She was being ridden by a policeman in a blue uniform. He had friendly blue eyes and a sandy mustache.

"You wouldn't believe it, but your horse looks just like my horse," Stevie said to the policeman. "It's uncanny. My horse has the same color coat, the same eyes. The only difference is that Belle has short socks on the right and long socks on the left. Our horses are opposites."

"Where's your horse?" asked the policeman.

"Back home in—" Stevie suddenly stopped. She didn't want this policeman to know that she came from Virginia. Then he would want to know how she had gotten here. And if she told him she came with a school group, he would want to know where the rest of the group was.

Stevie took a deep breath. "Belle is home on my grandfather's ranch."

"And where's that?" asked the policeman.

"Idaho," said Stevie. Chances were that the policeman didn't know much about Idaho.

"Why aren't you in school?" the policeman asked.

"I'm on vacation," Stevie said. She could tell that the policeman didn't really believe her, but she wasn't actually breaking the law. Still, she thought the sooner she got out of there, the better.

"I'm meeting my grandfather," she said. "I like to ride on the carousel over and over and over again, and he gets bored. So he dropped me off, and he's going to pick me up."

The policeman nodded. His blue eyes shined. "When I was a kid I liked to go on that carousel, too." He smiled as he remembered. "I grew up here in the city. The carousel horses were the only horses I ever rode." He looked at the carousel, which had started up again. "It was just the same then as it is now. Nothing has changed."

"My favorite is the black one," Stevie said. "I call him Ralph."

"Good name," said the policeman. "So, where's your grandfather?"

"He's kind of a slow walker," she said. "He was thrown from a bucking bronco when he was young. He's a fantastic rider, but not like he was before the accident."

"I'd like to meet him," said the policeman. "He sounds like an interesting man."

Stevie looked around desperately. It was getting later and later. She had to get back to the museum.

"There he is," Stevie said. "Right over there." She pointed at the stream of people moving down the road. "I'm late. Gotta go! Great talking to you!" She dashed off.

"I GUESS WE should watch the news," Lisa said.

"Why?" said Carole. "So we can see how foolish we look?"

Carole and Lisa had just come back from Pine Hollow. They were rummaging in Carole's refrigerator for a snack.

Colonel Hanson's head popped around the corner. "Did I hear you say you were going to be on TV?"

"It's no big deal," said Carole.

"It's a really *small* deal," said Lisa.

"You girls are just being modest," Carole's father said. "If you're on television, I want to see it."

"No you don't," said Lisa.

Colonel Hanson shook his head. "It's good to be modest, but there's no point in overdoing it."

Lisa and Carole exchanged miserable looks. "We're not being modest," Lisa said. "We *were* horrible."

"As if you girls could ever be horrible," Colonel Hanson said happily. "What time are you on?"

"We're on the local news," Carole said glumly, "in five minutes."

"I know it's almost dinnertime, but this calls for popcorn," said Colonel Hanson. It was a Hanson family tradition that great movies and great TV called for great popcorn. "I'm going to make it with extra butter. You girls take care of the lemonade."

Lisa got the lemonade out of the refrigerator while Carole put glasses on a tray. As Lisa poured the lemonade, she said, "Don't you think we should warn him?"

"What are we going to tell him?" Carole asked miserably.

Silently they carried the tray into the TV room and sat on the couch.

"WCTV is my favorite news station," Colonel Hanson said. "They really tell it like it is."

Lisa and Carole sank onto the couch.

"Hey, have some popcorn while it's hot," Colonel Hanson said as he settled into his favorite chair.

"I'm saving it for later," Lisa said. Suddenly she didn't feel like eating.

Colonel Hanson picked up the remote and turned on the television. Cheerful marching music played while WCTV's logo appeared on the screen. An announcer described the top two stories of the day, and then he said, "Today, Melody Manners is bringing us the first in a series called 'Genius Kids.' Melody?" He turned to her with a smile.

Melody said, "Today we're going to be meeting a very special kid, a rider who understands that it isn't all horse shows and prize ribbons. Taking care of tack is important, too."

"That's you, Carole," Colonel Hanson said. He settled back happily into his chair.

Carole sank even lower on the couch.

Veronica appeared on the screen as Melody said, "Veronica diAngelo is a serious rider. She knows that taking care of her horse and her equipment comes first."

"Veronica?" said Colonel Hanson. "Whoever decided she was a Genius Kid?"

"Veronica's father is friendly with the man who owns the television station," said Carole.

Colonel Hanson put his hands behind his head. "That's too bad."

"You're telling me," said Lisa. "Carole ought to be the Genius Kid."

The three of them watched while Carole stripped the

saddle, and Veronica explained to Melody what she was doing.

"Nice work," Colonel Hanson said. "I know an expert job when I see one."

They watched while Carole washed the inside of the saddle and dried it.

Colonel Hanson beamed proudly.

They watched while Carole washed and dried the seat and the flaps of the saddle, and Veronica kept on talking.

"That's not so bad," Colonel Hanson said.

"Just wait," Lisa said darkly.

On the TV set Melody suggested that Veronica polish the seat of the saddle herself. Onscreen, Veronica looked panicked for a second, then reached for a tin of black leather polish.

"Not that one!" yelled Colonel Hanson. Even on TV it was obvious that Veronica was picking up the wrong tin.

With a satisfied smile, Veronica opened the tin, plunged in her sponge, and made a black line across the saddle.

"She ruined a beautiful new saddle!" cried Colonel Hanson.

"There's more," said Lisa.

On the TV, Lisa said it was her fault. And then Carole said it was her fault. And then they started scrubbing at the black streak.

"I've got to hand it to you girls," Colonel Hanson said.

"We're the biggest idiots on earth, right?" said Lisa.

"Wrong," said Colonel Hanson. "You were thinking about Pine Hollow. You didn't want the stable to look bad."

For a second Lisa was filled with pride. But then she thought about what the kids at school would say. "We'll never hear the end of this. We acted so dumb. Kids will be teasing us for years."

Carole nodded and crossed her arms. Lisa knew that Carole couldn't stand the idea of people thinking she had damaged a saddle so senselessly.

"Nonsense," Colonel Hanson said. "You two are heroes."

"Heroes?" said Carole.

"You thought of others, not of yourselves," said Colonel Hanson. "If you were Marines, you'd get medals."

"The worst part is that WCTV is coming back tomorrow to tape Veronica—make that *us*—cleaning a bridle. This is shaping up as the worst vacation ever," Lisa said.

"You know what we need?" Carole asked.

Lisa shook her head.

"A good laugh," said Carole

"All we need is something to laugh at," Lisa said.

36

"Let's call Stevie. She can tell us about her glamorous visit to New York," Carole said.

"Yes!" said Lisa. "If anyone can cheer us up, it's Stevie."

Carole found the name and phone number of the hotel where Stevie's class was staying in New York. "This is going to be fun," she said. She dialed the hotel and asked for Stevie's room.

Lisa ran into the next room for the extension.

After two rings the phone in New York was picked up. "Hello?" said Stevie.

"Stevie!" said Lisa and Carole at the same time.

"We need you!" said Carole.

"Tell us something funny," said Lisa.

A woman's voice said, "I'm sorry. Stevie can't come to the phone."

"But she already came to the phone," Lisa said.

The phone went dead.

Lisa and Carole stared at each other. What was going on?

"PLEASE STOP CRYING," Stevie said. "It makes me feel terrible."

She and Ms. Dodge were in Stevie's hotel room. The rest of the class had gone to dinner and then to see a play. Stevie had to stay at the hotel as punishment.

That afternoon Stevie had dashed back to the museum, rushed into the gift shop, and grabbed a postcard. She paid quickly and stuffed it in a bag, thinking that everything would be fine.

But Mrs. Martin asked each of them to show their postcard and explain why they had chosen their particular object.

One girl had chosen a ruffled ballgown from the costume wing. Another had chosen a violin. Another had chosen an antique valentine card with cupids and lace. Everyone had good explanations for their choices.

And then it was Stevie's turn. Stevie reached into the bag, hoping that she had grabbed something good. It was a portrait of a very tall woman with a slightly red nose.

"Good selection, Stevie," said Mrs. Martin. "Why did you choose it?"

Usually, Stevie had no trouble thinking up explanations, but this time she was almost stumped. "I like that nose," she said. "Most artists would pretend it wasn't pink. They'd paint it white."

"Good point," said Mrs. Martin. "I can see you've given this a lot of thought. How would you describe this artist's place in American art?"

That was a toughie, since Stevie had no idea who the artist was.

"It's an important position," Stevie said. "American art wouldn't be what it is without him."

"Stevie," said Mrs. Martin, crossing her arms. "What's the artist's name?"

"It's on the tip of my tongue," Stevie said. She tried to peek at the back of the postcard to see if the name was printed there.

"No, it's not," said Mrs. Martin. "His name is John Singer Sargent. It's obvious to me, Stevie, that you were fooling around in the store. You didn't choose an object at all."

"I was not fooling around in the store," Stevie said.

"Then what were you doing?" asked Mrs. Martin.

Stevie had realized that if Mrs. Martin found out what she had really been doing, she would be in the biggest trouble of her life. She would blow her chance to make up her grades, and she would lose her riding privileges. So she had said that the store was lots of fun. That wasn't a lie exactly. The store *was* lots of fun. But she hadn't spent any time there.

Now she was being punished. She had to miss a fancy dinner and the theater. She couldn't make or receive phone calls, which was bad because she couldn't call Skye to tell him where she was staying.

But that wasn't the worst of it. Ms. Dodge had been looking forward to the play that night. It was from a book by her favorite author, Henry James. And now she was upset.

"I am the world's biggest jerk," said Stevie. She felt really guilty. Ms. Dodge was a little quiet but very nice. Sometimes she even laughed at Stevie's jokes, and she was always willing to help students. *She'd never ruin someone's trip,* Stevie thought bitterly.

"You aren't a jerk," Ms. Dodge said, wiping her eyes. "You have a good heart, Stevie, but you get carried away."

"I ruined your trip," Stevie said.

"No, you didn't," Ms. Dodge said. "This gives us a chance to spend time together. I'm sorry I got upset. I'm a little disappointed, but we'll have fun."

Stevie wished Ms. Dodge would just get mad. The nicer she acted, the worse Stevie felt.

"I can't understand why you don't hate me," Stevie said.

"I like you," Ms. Dodge said quietly.

"Ugh," said Stevie, throwing herself into a chair. "I hate myself."

"Stevie, you have to realize that what you did this afternoon was wrong," said Ms. Dodge.

*She knows!* Stevie thought. *She knows I was running all over the park.*

"Mrs. Martin gave this trip a lot of thought," Ms. Dodge said. "She wanted to give you all as much freedom as possible. She wanted each of you to pick out an object on your own and research it on your own. But you didn't do that, Stevie. You wasted time in the store.

"I know museum stores are fun," Ms. Dodge continued, "but you didn't do your job. And your grades are in jeopardy."

"I always seem to get in trouble when I don't really mean to," Stevie said, shaking her head. "I guess I should really shape up."

Ms. Dodge went over to Stevie and sat on the arm of her chair. "You're growing up, Stevie. You have to stop acting like a little kid."

Stevie thought for a minute. "I'm going to change," she said with determination. "From now on I am going to be thoughtful and cooperative. Ms. Dodge, you are going to be proud of me."

Ms. Dodge nodded. "I know I will, Stevie. I have faith in you. I think this trip to New York is going to be a real growing experience for you."

Stevie resolved that she would never, ever act like a jerk again. And the next day, if she was really good, she'd get her phone privileges back. Then she'd be able to call Skye Ransom. And then she'd take Ms. Dodge backstage to see the real, true glamour of New York City.

WHEN SHE WOKE ON Thursday morning, Stevie knew something was wrong, but she couldn't remember what it was. She sat in bed, stretching her arms.

Then she remembered that she'd promised to behave all day. That thought was so depressing that she lay down and pulled the covers over her head. "Woe is me," she groaned.

"Are you sick?" asked Helen, Stevie's roommate.

If this had been an average day, Stevie would have pretended that she'd caught some vile disease. But she realized that wouldn't work. Besides, she'd be going back on her promise. She pulled the covers from her face and said, "No, I'm not sick. I'm fine. But thank you for asking."

"Are you sure you're okay, Stevie?" Helen said. "You don't sound like yourself."

"I'm fine," Stevie said, walking toward the bathroom. "Yes, today is a very fine day, and I'm lucky to be alive."

Inside the bathroom, Stevie scrubbed her teeth. Then she saw Helen's travel bag. It had not just toothpaste but dental floss. A really disciplined person would floss her teeth right now.

"Is it okay if I use your dental floss?" Stevie called.

"Are aliens inhabiting your body?" Helen replied. "This can't be the real Stevie."

Stevie flossed her teeth. When she was done, she thought of how pleased her dentist would be.

Stevie brushed her hair fifty strokes. She had read somewhere that this would produce perfect hair. All it did was turn her ears pink, but it made her feel virtuous.

When Stevie looked in her suitcase, she knew she would have trouble finding something good to wear. She had stuffed it with black clothes because she'd read that the hip people in New York only wear black. She pulled out a black turtleneck. "Disgusting," she said. She pulled out a pair of black jeans. "What poor taste." She found black socks and a black sweater. "Revolting."

At the bottom of the suitcase was a flowered dress.

Stevie's mother must have sneaked it in there at the last moment. Stevie was her mother's only daughter, and she knew that Mrs. Lake had dreams that someday Stevie would wear a dress.

"My mom is so thoughtful," said Stevie, pulling the dress out of the suitcase. She looked at the flowers on the dress. "How did she know that petunias are my favorites?"

"I think you've gone mad, Stevie," said her roommate.

"That shows what you know," Stevie huffed.

At breakfast, Stevie sat next to Ms. Dodge, who told her how nice she looked. Ms. Dodge ordered an English muffin with "a smidgen of strawberry jam." Stevie had been planning on loading up on sausages, eggs, and waffles. But she figured she'd have an easier time being good if she didn't overeat, so she ordered an English muffin herself.

After breakfast they went to the Museum of American Folk Art to see samplers and other embroidery. Ms. Dodge explained that well-born ladies used to spend whole days sewing.

"Think of that," Stevie said, peering at an embroidery of a willow tree. "You could go blind doing that." When she noticed that Ms. Dodge was listening, she added, "Not that it wouldn't be worth it."

The class had lunch at a restaurant near Lincoln Center. Stevie sat next to Ms. Dodge. She was starving, but she ordered what Ms. Dodge ordered—a watercress and cream cheese sandwich with the crusts cut off.

"Hey," Stevie said. "And I always thought watercress was stringy and dull."

"Watercress is the queen of leafy greens," said Ms. Dodge, patting her lips with her napkin.

After lunch they headed uptown toward the New-York Historical Society. Stevie walked with Ms. Dodge, who was fascinated by the dresses in the store windows.

"Isn't that lovely?" said Ms. Dodge, pointing to a cream silk dress. "It's so elegant."

All Stevie could think was *Spots*. If she wore that dress it would be covered with spots in no time. She sneaked a look at Ms. Dodge, who didn't have a single spot on her clothes.

Stevie imagined herself without spots. She saw herself with perfectly groomed hair. Strangely, she looked a little like Veronica diAngelo.

They crossed Central Park South and entered the park at the southeast corner. Stevie heard a familiar *clop*, *clop* noise. *Horses*, she thought, smiling.

"I do love the fragile quality of early spring light," Ms. Dodge said.

"*Fragile* is the word," Stevie said.

Stevie heard the cawing of a crow. In Willow Creek crows were not particularly popular. There were too many of them, and they made a lot of noise. But here the crow's cawing made Stevie long for the open fields of Willow Creek. One crow rose from a tree. It was joined by another crow. And then another. Cawing and squabbling, they flew north.

From far off, Stevie thought she could hear tinny carousel music. She thought of the man with the backward hat who worked at the carousel. That was an okay job—running the carousel, making sure everyone was safe. She figured he was having a good time right now.

Stevie thought of the mounted policeman. He would be riding through the park finding lost children, telling tourists where to go for the best french fries. That was a *really* great job.

"I know you'll do really well today, Stevie," said Ms. Dodge. "You're behind the rest of the class. You haven't selected an object, but I know you'll find something splendid."

"You can count on me," Stevie said, remembering her resolution to be good.

A horse-drawn carriage passed. In the back were a young man and woman holding hands and staring into each other's eyes. Stevie thought of Phil, her boyfriend. If he had been here, they'd have been having a good time. She sighed. She had been doing okay until her class entered the park, but now she could feel her goodness wearing thin.

The New-York Historical Society was an austere marble building on Central Park West. The class trooped up the outside marble steps. Inside were more marble steps. *The guy who designed this building was certainly into steps*, Stevie thought.

Mrs. Martin clapped her hands, a signal that the group should draw around her in a ring. "Today I want you to find objects that go with your special object," she said. "You can buy postcards in the store on the main floor. You have two hours. Everyone will meet in the lobby at four."

Stevie trudged up more marble stairs. When she got to the top floor, she looked around.

"There are so many wonderful things here," Ms. Dodge said. "I know you'll find a perfect object." She gave Stevie an encouraging smile.

Stevie walked into the first room. It had chairs, silver teapots, and cups and saucers. "You could die of excitement," she muttered to herself. She caught Ms. Dodge looking at her and smiled. "Great stuff," she said. "Those cups and saucers are something else."

Stevie walked into another room. *Hey, more chairs*. Over a chest of drawers was an oil painting of a horse. Stevie stepped closer to look at it. The horse was running, but in a very odd way. Both front legs were straight out, and both hind legs were straight back. A horse that ran like that would fall flat on its stomach.

But so what? The horse was running. (Or floating, to be more accurate.) His nose was up, his tail was out. Stevie could hear the thunder of hoofbeats. She could feel the wind in her hair. Suddenly she wanted to ride the carousel again.

Stevie looked at Ms. Dodge, who was gazing at a teapot with an expression of rapture. Then she looked at the door. It would be so easy to disappear. It wouldn't be good, but it would be easy. She looked at Ms. Dodge again. She had moved on to a coffeepot.

Stevie slipped out the door. Softly she ran down the marble steps. On the main floor she paused. She shouldn't do this, she knew. She should stay in the museum. She should find an object. On the other hand, outside the air was fresh, the crows were flying, and Ralph was waiting for a nice chat.

Stevie stepped out the door.

"TODAY'S OUR LUCKY day," Lisa said miserably.

"Not," Carole said gloomily.

They were in the tack room at the stable. They'd gotten there early in case there was anything Max wanted them to do before Veronica gave her lecture on bridle care.

Veronica walked in from the barn. There was a white paper bag in her pocket.

"Hey, you're early," Lisa said. She had never known Veronica to be early for anything.

"Have you got a problem with that?" Veronica said snootily. She looked Carole and Lisa up and down. "Why don't you find Max?" she said. "He may want you for something."

Lisa and Carole didn't like being bossed by Veronica. On the other hand, looking for Max had the distinct advantage of getting them away from Veronica. They walked into the barn to find him.

Max was mucking out a stall.

"Is there anything we can do?" Carole said.

"You've already done a lot," Max said. "You were great yesterday."

"Anything for Pine Hollow," Carole said with a grin.

"I appreciate it," Max said. He raked the stall so that the earth was higher in the center than it was at the sides. "I hope everything goes more smoothly today," he said. He hung the rake on a hook, and the three of them went off to join Veronica.

When they entered the tack room, Veronica was bent over the container of cleaning supplies. Lisa and Carole exchanged surprised looks. Was Veronica actually trying to learn about cleaning tack?

There was the sound of wheels in the mud outside.

"They're here," Veronica said cheerfully. "I know today is going to be wonderful."

Melody came into the room with the cameraman. "We got a lot of good feedback about yesterday," she said. "Who knew that cleaning a saddle could be so dramatic? I nearly fainted when you put that black polish on the saddle."

"It wasn't my fault," Veronica said stiffly.

Lisa realized that Veronica actually believed that the mixup with the polish had been Lisa and Carole's fault. She figured that there were some people who just couldn't admit when they were wrong, even to themselves. She decided the best thing to do was to stay away from Veronica, so she stepped to the side. A patch of white in the wastebasket caught her eye. Casually she leaned over and looked. It was the white bag that Veronica had been carrying. It said JERRY'S JOKE SHOP. Lisa felt a sense of dread.

"Okay, guys," Melody said. "Let's get started. And don't worry about mistakes. Just plunge on ahead."

Veronica pointed to the hook where her bridle was hanging.

"That's some bridle," Melody said, her voice filled with awe. The bridle had two reins on each side and two different bits. "Tell me about it."

"It's a double bridle. My father gave it to me, and, of course, it's custom-made," said Veronica. There was an uncomfortable pause when Veronica clearly couldn't think of anything else to say.

"The bit with two pieces is a bridoon or snaffle," Carole whispered.

"This is the bridoon," said Veronica, pointing to the bit that was made of two pieces of metal hooked together. "It's also called a snaffle."

"What's the other bit called?" asked Melody.

"It's called a bit or curb," whispered Carole.

"This is a bit," said Veronica. The second bit was a single piece of metal with a curve in the center. "Note the two pairs of hand-sewn reins."

"And when do you use this type of bridle?" Melody asked.

"This type of bridle is used for advanced training, particularly in dressage," said Veronica. "And now," she added with a smile, "Carole will clean the bridle, and Lisa will polish it."

Carole removed the bits and curb chain and put them in a bucket of water. "I'm stripping it," Carole whispered.

"Carole is stripping the bridle," Veronica said.

Carole undid the lip strap, then she undid all the buckles and moved them to the lowest holes. She washed the leather with a wet sponge.

"Carole has washed the bridle. Lisa is going to dry it," said Veronica.

Lisa picked up a chamois cloth. It was soft, the way it was supposed to be, but it also felt itchy. Her fingertips felt as if they were on fire. *"Orrrf,"* she said, dropping the cloth.

Carole dived for it. She stood up, looking relieved. An expression of surprise crossed her face. "Eccch," she said.

Lisa couldn't let this happen to Carole. She grabbed the cloth. Her whole hand itched now, and so did her arm.

"Lisa is supposed to be drying the bridle," Veronica said. "But she seems to be having difficulty. I guess she's suffering from nerves."

Lisa wouldn't let Pine Hollow down. She started to dry the bridle with the cloth. But the more she dried the bridle, the more her fingers itched. She thought of the white bag from the joke shop. Could Veronica have covered the chamois cloth with itching powder?

Carole could see that Lisa was having trouble. She wanted to help. "I'll do it," she said, reaching for the cloth.

Lisa couldn't let her do that. "No," she said.

"I insist," Carole said, grabbing for the cloth.

"Now, girls," Veronica said. "We mustn't compete."

"I'll take it," Lisa said a little more firmly.

"No, me," said Carole, pulling at one side.

Carole and Lisa pulled at opposite ends of the cloth.

"A little bit of attention and they lose control," Veronica said smugly.

Lisa lost her grip on the cloth. Carole lost hers at the same time. The chamois cloth fell into the bucket of water.

"I'll get another," Max said. He opened a drawer and pulled out a fresh cloth. When he handed it to Lisa, he gave her an odd look.

"Do you think you girls can cooperate now?" said Veronica.

Carole's face was pink. Lisa could tell that she was so angry that she was on the verge of tears.

"Yes, we can, Veronica," Lisa said. She dried the noseband and the reins. Then she gave the cloth to Carole.

"Very good," said Veronica. "It's nice to see you two getting along for a change."

STEVIE CROSSED THE STREET into Central Park. She hadn't given up on being good. She was just . . . taking a break.

Finding the carousel was not as easy as she'd thought. First she wound up at an ice-skating rink, and then at something called the Dairy. Finally she heard the lovely, tinny music of the carousel.

She came around the corner and saw that there was no line at all. That was great. She'd buy a ticket, hop on, hop off, and be back at the historical society before anyone missed her.

"One ticket," she said to the fuzzy-haired man.

"Just one?" he said with a smile.

Stevie realized that his business must not be too good at the moment. She owed it to him to buy more than one ticket. "I'll have two," she said. "Well, actually, three."

He counted out the tickets and said, "Enjoy."

"I believe I will," Stevie said with a grin.

When the carousel music had stopped playing and the gate was opened, Stevie went in. To her delight, she saw that there was no one on Ralph. She climbed on and leaned toward his head. "Did you miss me?" she said.

Ralph didn't reply.

"I missed you," she said.

The man with the backward baseball hat came to take her ticket. "You don't have to buckle up today," he said. "I realize you're an experienced rider."

For a second Stevie felt like telling him about Belle and how she missed her horse—and about the class trip and all the horrible antiques. But he was already on his way to take another ticket. She held on to the pole, waiting for the music to start. She looked up, waiting for the horse to rise with the music. On the other side of the carousel fence, she saw the mounted policeman. He was staring at her. Ralph started moving.

"Go, Ralph," she said, leaning slightly forward, the way she did when she wanted Belle to go faster. "We're in big trouble. We'd better get out of here."

But Ralph just went around and around and around.

"Ralph," she said, "you're a great horse, but you have one shortcoming. You're no good for escapes."

Ralph sank lower and lower. Stevie thought of sliding off Ralph's back and sneaking away, but she realized she couldn't do that. The carousel was surrounded by a stout iron fence. "If you weren't attached to this carousel, you could jump the fence and we could gallop away together," she said.

Ralph started moving up.

The policeman had his hands on the pommel of his saddle. Stevie could tell that he was planning to wait until she got off the carousel.

For a second Stevie had visions of jail. She saw herself behind bars. Then she reminded herself that they don't put kids in jail for playing hooky from a school trip. On the other hand, if she returned to the historical society in the custody of the police, she would be in big trouble.

As the carousel whirled around and around, Stevie's mind also whirled. She was in a tough spot, one of the toughest of her life. She had to do something, but what?

The music slowed and the carousel wound to a stop. Ahead of her a mother lifted a child from a horse and put him on the ground. The two of them walked toward the exit.

Stevie had a brilliant idea. She'd hide among the mothers and children. As she walked toward the exit, she bent her knees. She wasn't as short as the kids, but she was semishort.

She crept through the gate and past the ticket booth. She turned right, ready to straighten up and run for Central Park West. There was a shadow in her path. She looked up.

The policeman looked down at her. "Do you have trouble with your knees?" he asked.

"You won't believe it," said Stevie, straightening up. "Some people have one trick knee, but I have two."

"I'm sorry to hear it," the policeman said. "Do you have some identification?"

Stevie thought fast. Her home address and phone number were in her wallet. If the policeman got her phone number, he'd call her parents and she'd be grounded for the rest of her life.

"My grandfather has it," Stevie said. "He's meeting me here." She looked around. "He's late again. But that's him. Absentminded."

"What's your name?" the policeman said.

Stevie thought fast. "Jane Jones." The name didn't even sound real.

"Your grandfather should be more careful. You shouldn't be wandering around alone. You might get lost," the policeman said.

"What can I do?" Stevie said. "It's my grandfather. He has all these strange notions."

The policeman pulled his walkie-talkie from his belt. "I'm worried about you," he said. "I'm going to call for a car to come and get you. I don't want you wandering around Central Park by yourself."

He said something in a low voice into the walkie-talkie.

Stevie figured that this was it. Her life was ending.

Over the top of the hill came a swarm of skaters wearing black helmets and knee pads. They were bent low, swinging their arms. The wheels of their skates made a faint whir as they raced along.

The policeman's horse snorted and backed up. A skater stumbled and rocketed toward the horse. The horse whinnied with fear, and the skater screamed.

Stevie stepped away. The policeman was watching the skater, who was watching the policeman. Stevie looked over her shoulder. The park was green and welcoming and safe. She started running. She ran past a flower bed and a row of benches. A man lying on a bench looked up at her with surprise. She realized that she was drawing attention to herself by running and forced herself to walk. It was the hardest thing she had ever done. Her feet wanted to fly. Her arms wanted to pump.

*Go slowly*, she told herself. *Look casual. Act cool.*

There was a shout.

*That's it*, she thought.

*"Look out!"* came a familiar voice.

Stevie saw a baseball zooming toward her. She put her hands up to protect herself, and the ball landed in her hands.

"Great catch," said the voice. Under the brim of a baseball hat was the friendly face of Skye Ransom. "Stevie!" he said. "I've been waiting to hear from you. How come you didn't call?"

"I'm kind of in trouble," she said. "I can't make phone calls."

"Same old Stevie," said Skye with a grin. "Always up to something."

*If he only knew*, Stevie thought.

"I'm in a rush," Stevie said, looking over her shoulder. "But I'm staying at the New Gotham Hotel with some kids from my class."

"A lot of kids?" said Skye, looking worried.

"Only six and two teachers," Stevie said.

"I can get hold of eight tickets," Skye said. "Come to my show tonight. You'll come backstage, and then I'll take you guys out to dinner."

"Great!" Stevie said.

"Want to join our team?" Skye said. "We can use your talent. That was some catch."

"I wish," Stevie said. Veronica would *die* if she heard that Stevie had played in the Broadway Show League. On the other hand, Stevie would probably die if she

59

didn't get back to the historical society. "Unfortunately, I've got to run!" she said.

"But—" Skye said.

"We'll catch up later," Stevie said.

"Wait!" Skye said.

A group of tourists with cameras was passing. "Are you Skye Ransom?" one of them said to him.

"That's what they tell me," he said with a grin.

As tourists surrounded Skye, Stevie blended into the group. She didn't want to risk having the policeman spot her. When the tourists finished taking pictures, she walked with them toward Central Park West.

On Central Park West she figured she was far enough away from the policeman that she could hustle. She dog-trotted all the way to the historical society.

She ran up the marble steps and into the lobby of the society's building with one minute to spare. Then she dashed into the store and looked at the post-cards. She had to get a postcard of an object that was not a painting. If it was a painting, she would have to know all about the artist. She noticed one of a lamp with a glass shade. *Lamps don't have artists. They're just lamps*, she thought. She bought the post-card and went out to the lobby to wait for the rest of her group.

She had just stopped panting when Mrs. Martin appeared. "I hope you did a better job today, Stevie," she said.

"Much better," Stevie said.

The rest of the group had gathered.

"Show us what you picked," Mrs. Martin said.

Stevie pulled the postcard of the glass lamp out of the bag. "Is that a lamp or what?" she said. "I'm not too into antiques, but I could live with this lamp."

"Tell us something about it," Mrs. Martin said.

"It's like a plant," Stevie said. "It has branches, roots, flowers. . . . It's like a living thing, almost."

"Very good," Mrs. Martin said. "Who made it?"

What kind of a question was that? "A lamp maker," Stevie said.

A line of irritation appeared between Mrs. Martin's eyes. "I cannot believe you selected this object without knowing who made it."

"I'll find out later," Stevie said. "This lamp and I are connected."

"Then you would want to know that it's made by Louis Comfort Tiffany," said Mrs. Martin.

"He's an American genius," said Ms. Dodge.

"There's a whole exhibit of those lamps upstairs," said Mrs. Martin. "How could you have picked a Tiffany lamp as your object without seeing the exhibit?"

Stevie felt her face turn red. Truly, she had blown it. Again.

"You've been fooling around all this time," Mrs. Martin said. "You've been hanging out in the store."

"Absolutely not," Stevie said.

"Then where were you?" asked Mrs. Martin.

Stevie realized that she had to think faster than she had ever thought before. She thought of Skye. She thought of the tickets. She thought of the backstage visit. She thought of a nice hearty meal. She knew that Skye would make a good excuse for her disappearance.

"It's like this," she said. "I couldn't talk on the phone last night, so I couldn't call this friend of mine who's a movie star."

Mrs. Martin sighed and looked away.

"He's not just a movie star, he's also a Broadway star," Stevie said. "He's in *Murder at Midnight*. He's going to give us all free tickets, invite us backstage afterward, and introduce us to stars. And then he's going to take us out to dinner. And then he'll take us home in a limousine."

Mrs. Martin shook her head. "When we get back to Willow Creek, I am going to have a long, long talk with your parents."

"You don't have to make up stories like that," said Ms.

Dodge. "I know maybe you feel insecure sometimes, Stevie, but it's better to tell the truth."

"It *is* the truth," Stevie said. "Wait until we get back to the hotel. Tickets will be waiting for us."

Mrs. Martin and Ms. Dodge looked at each other and sighed.

By the time Lisa and Carole got to Carole's house, they were exhausted.

"Scratching really wears you out," said Lisa as she rubbed her elbow.

"What made that cloth so itchy?" Carole said.

"Itching powder," said Lisa.

"What's that?" Carole said.

"You buy it at joke shops," Lisa said. "My cousin Albert is always buying stuff like itching powder. He also likes plastic ice cubes with flies inside."

"He sounds like a million laughs," Carole said.

"You don't know the half of it." Lisa groaned. "Anyway, when we first saw Veronica, she had a white bag in her pocket. Later the bag was in the wastebasket. It was from Jerry's Joke Shop."

"That's why she told us to go help Max," Carole said. "She wanted a chance to put itching powder on the chamois cloth."

"Exactly," Lisa said. "She knew we'd wind up making total fools of ourselves."

"And we did," said Carole. "How come Veronica always seems to win?"

"Because Stevie isn't here," Lisa said. "We need her diabolical brain."

"I bet she's having a fantastic time in New York," said Carole.

"While Veronica tortures us in Virginia," said Lisa.

Twenty minutes later the girls had showered and shampooed and put on fresh clothes. The itching was gone.

"Let's have a snack," Lisa said.

There were fresh chocolate chip cookies in the cookie jar. Lisa put some on a plate while Carole poured glasses of milk.

"Maybe Melody will lose the videotape and we won't be on TV," said Lisa.

"Somehow I have the feeling that she won't," said Carole.

From the front of the house came the sound of a door opening. "I'm home," came Colonel Hanson's voice. He walked into the kitchen. "Are you on TV again?"

"Yes, and it'll be worse," Carole said. "We looked like even bigger dummies."

"Wait until you see," said Lisa.

Colonel Hanson turned on the news. The top story was the weather. "There's good news," the meteorologist said. "The storm that has been drenching Willow Creek is finally moving up the coast. By tomorrow the sun will be shining here, and New York City will have our rain."

"Poor Stevie," Carole said. "It's no fun being a tourist in the rain."

"Stevie will cope," Colonel Hanson said with a grin. "She always finds a way."

Carole crossed her arms, thinking that somehow she and Lisa never seemed to find a way.

In the "Genius Kid" segment, Veronica looked as beautifully groomed as a movie star. Her black hair was shining. Her nails and lips were red. Her skin was creamy.

Veronica explained about a bridoon and a Weymouth bit and why her bridle had four reins.

"She knows a thing or two," said Colonel Hanson, clearly impressed.

"I was whispering the facts to her," Carole said. "She doesn't know a thing."

66

They watched as Carole stripped the bridle and then washed it.

"You girls really do deserve medals," said Colonel Hanson.

Then Veronica said that Lisa was going to dry the bridle. Lisa picked up the chamois cloth and her face suddenly got a very odd look. The cloth flew out of her hands. Carole grabbed it. Next thing, the girls seemed to be fighting over it while Veronica told them to share.

Colonel Hanson watched in silence. When it was over, he said, "Itching powder?"

"You know about itching powder?" Lisa asked.

Colonel Hanson nodded. "When I was a new recruit there was a guy in my platoon who used to like stuff like itching powder."

"And ice cubes with flies in them?" asked Lisa.

"Exactly," said Colonel Hanson. "That guy had the worst sense of humor of anyone I ever knew. He drove us all crazy."

"Was his name Albert?" Lisa asked.

"No, Virgil," said Colonel Hanson.

"Oh no, there are two of them out there," Lisa moaned.

Colonel Hanson thought for a minute. "What did Max do?" he finally asked.

"Nothing," said Lisa.

Colonel Hanson nodded. "Max is no dope. He knows

67

what's going on. I'm sure he's got some kind of plan. Just hang in there."

"But we always wind up looking like creeps," Lisa wailed.

"I don't think so," Colonel Hanson said. "Trust me."

"THIS IS NOT only unfair," Stevie said, "it's inhuman."

Tickets for Skye's show had arrived at the hotel, but Mrs. Martin wouldn't let Stevie go.

"I told you Skye was going to send tickets, and he did," Stevie said. "Nobody believed me, but I was right. So why can't I go?"

"Because you still haven't been taking this trip seriously," said Mrs. Martin. "You haven't been the least bit cooperative."

Stevie opened her mouth, about to argue with Mrs. Martin, but then she realized that if Mrs. Martin knew what she had *really* been doing, she would be in trouble for life. "I guess you're right," she said miserably.

Mrs. Martin looked down at the tickets in her hand. "It's true that Skye Ransom is your friend, Stevie. Without you we never would have gotten these tickets. If you like, I can return them to Mr. Ransom."

"No way!" Stevie said. "His play sounds fantastic. There are thrills. There are chills. Plus, Skye is a great actor."

"You're a nice person, Stevie," said Mrs. Martin. "You're generous and sweet. But you have no discipline. You have no inner fiber. You'll never get anyplace unless you change."

"She will," said Ms. Dodge, putting her arm around Stevie. "I know she'll do better."

"But Ms. Dodge will have to stay and watch me," Stevie groaned. "It's really not fair. She's going to miss two plays in a row. I'm single-handedly wrecking her trip to New York."

"I don't mind staying," Ms. Dodge said. "It will give us a chance to spend some time together."

*If only Ms. Dodge weren't so nice*, Stevie thought. She was making Stevie feel miserable.

"We'll have a good time," Ms. Dodge said to Stevie. "We'll order dinner from room service and then we'll watch TV."

Stevie crumpled. This did *not* sound like a fantastic evening. "I've always wanted to go backstage at a Broadway show," she said to Mrs. Martin. "It's a lifelong dream. I promise . . ."

Mrs. Martin shook her head. "I'm sorry, Stevie."

When the class had gone, Ms. Dodge got the room service menu and said, "What would you like, Stevie?"

"Bread and water," Stevie said miserably.

"Don't be like that," said Ms. Dodge with a smile. "Take a look at the menu."

On the menu there were good things like hamburgers and fries. And there was an array of tempting desserts. But Stevie knew that somehow or other she had to get herself under control. No way was she going to wander off in the park again. Maybe eating right would help.

"What are you having?" she asked Ms. Dodge.

"The sautéed filet of sole looks scrumptious," said Ms. Dodge.

"Totally," said Stevie.

Ms. Dodge waggled her fingers over the menu as if she were having trouble deciding. "How about some broccoli to go with that fish?"

"Fantastic," Stevie said. Until this moment, she would rather have died than order broccoli.

Half an hour later, a man wheeled a table into their room. The plates were covered with metal domes to keep the food warm.

"Let's dig in," Ms. Dodge said happily.

When the waiter whipped the cover off her plate, Stevie nearly fainted. There was a slab of white fish, a *huge* pile of broccoli, and a sprig of parsley. *Well*, Stevie figured, *I can eat the parsley.*

But Ms. Dodge was so nice that Stevie didn't want to hurt her feelings. She scooped up a forkful of broccoli. She closed her eyes. She opened her mouth. She inserted the broccoli. She chewed. The broccoli didn't have a lot of taste, but it wasn't that bad, either. She opened her eyes with relief.

"Most kids don't like broccoli," said Ms. Dodge.

"I'm building my inner fiber," said Stevie with a chuckle.

"I'm glad you can laugh," said Ms. Dodge. "To tell you the truth, I was afraid this evening was going to be grim."

"This is the best broccoli I ever ate," Stevie said. "And to tell you the truth, it's the first broccoli I ever ate."

Ms. Dodge giggled. It was a very nice sound. Somehow it made Stevie feel better.

Stevie ate half the broccoli—she figured that eating more would be overdoing it. And then she looked at

the fish. The aunt who lived in a house full of antiques always ate fish. And her aunt was famous for
her good taste. Stevie told herself that *this* fish was a
whole new experience for her. *This* fish represented
adventure.

Stevie took a bite. The fish wasn't the greatest—it was
kind of limp—but it wasn't the worst, either. She told
herself to pretend that she was at TD's, eating one of her
famous ice cream concoctions.

It didn't work. The fish tasted like fish.

"You don't have to eat it all, Stevie," said Ms. Dodge
with a smile.

Stevie smiled back gratefully. She ate the parsley to
take away the taste of the fish.

When they were finished, they rolled the table out
into the hall.

"Room service is cool," Stevie said. "They've got everything figured out—how to keep the food warm, how
to get rid of the dirty dishes."

"They think ahead," said Ms. Dodge.

Stevie looked around the room. There wasn't much to
do but watch TV. "So what are your favorite shows?"
she asked.

"Let's see what's on the educational channel," Ms.
Dodge said.

Stevie had been hoping to catch an episode of *Range
Riders* because it had realistic horse-riding scenes, but

she figured that she should let Ms. Dodge choose the show. "Educational TV it is," she said.

Ms. Dodge switched the channel to a show about woodchucks—how they mated, how they reared their young. The woodchucks were cute, but somehow they didn't grab Stevie.

After a while, Stevie asked, "Could we watch something else?"

"Absolutely," said Ms. Dodge. "One of the nice things about New York is that there's more than one educational channel."

*Right*, Stevie thought.

"Here's something that might interest you," Ms. Dodge said. "The show is on Eadweard Muybridge, the photographer."

Stevie settled back in her chair, ready for pictures of sunsets or something like that. Instead she saw a photograph of a horse. It turned out that Muybridge took the first photographs of horses galloping.

"You're kidding me," Stevie said.

Ms. Dodge smiled.

Until Muybridge took his photographs, no one knew how horses galloped. This seemed kind of weird, but Stevie realized that horses gallop so fast that it's hard to see their legs. Until Muybridge, people thought that there was a moment when a horse had its back legs flying back and its front legs flying forward, with not a single hoof touching the ground.

"That explains that goofy picture of a horse in the historical society," Stevie said. "No one knew. This is really interesting."

It turned out that the only time a horse's feet leave the ground during a gallop is when all four feet are drawn together under the horse. This is called the moment of suspension.

"Wait until Lisa and Carole hear about Muybridge," Stevie said. "They'll be impressed."

"Educational television isn't always dull," Ms. Dodge said. "In fact, if you give it a chance, it's pretty interesting."

"This has been some evening, Ms. Dodge," Stevie said. "Broccoli. Fish. Educational television. I thought New York was going to be one glamorous treat after another, but everything has turned out the opposite." She thought a minute. "It's kind of fun, though. I'm seeing things I never saw before."

"There's a whole lot more you haven't seen," Ms. Dodge said. "There's a whole world out there."

Stevie thought about it. "When you think about adventure, you think about something you've never done before. And if it's broccoli—okay."

"You have a good spirit, Stevie," said Ms. Dodge.

"I'm going to be good from now on," Stevie said. Now that she was here, with Ms. Dodge, she realized how crazy she'd been to run around Central Park on her own. The policeman was right to be worried about her. *Sometimes I have no common sense*, Stevie thought. "It's going to be a whole new me," she said.

By ten-thirty, Stevie was eager for her class to come back from the theater so that she could show them how good she was.

The class didn't come.

By eleven she was dying for them to come back.

The class didn't come.

By eleven-thirty she was getting kind of grumpy.

By twelve she was getting steamed.

At twelve-twenty, the class returned. Mrs. Martin had spots of pink in her cheeks.

"How was the play?" asked Ms. Dodge.

"It was just a mystery," Mrs. Martin said. "It wasn't a serious play, but it wasn't half bad." She turned to Stevie. "Skye Ransom certainly can act."

"What a hunk," said one of Stevie's classmates with a sigh.

"*Hunk* is not a word we use," said Mrs. Martin, "unless we are talking about a piece of cheese."

"Was the mystery good?" asked Stevie wistfully.

"No one guessed the solution before the end," said Mrs. Martin. "It was really quite clever."

"You should see Skye's dressing room," one of the girls said to Stevie. "He has telegrams from stars—they all say 'Break a leg.' It's an old Broadway tradition."

"Were there lots of stars backstage?" Stevie said.

Helen shook her head. "Skye had a cousin there."

"So his cousin was glamorous?" Stevie said. She figured that movie stars must have outstanding cousins.

"He was nice," Helen said. "He's in junior high school. He likes math."

"I guess there was lots of food backstage," Stevie said. "Like incredible pastries."

"I saw a couple of paper cups of coffee," Helen said. "That's all."

Stevie had imagined the backstage filled with celebrities and fancy furniture and great food. Instead, it sounded kind of . . . ordinary.

"But Skye was great," Stevie said.

"The greatest," Cathy, one of the other girls, said. "He's making another horse movie. He said to tell you he'd write you a long letter about it."

"So dinner afterward was great," Stevie said.

"It was great," Cathy said. "But I'm not used to eating so late. I'm bushed." She gave a huge yawn.

"What about the limo?" said Stevie.

"It was good," Kim, another girl, said, yawning, too.

"People sure get used to glamour fast," said Stevie.

"Glamour isn't so . . . glamorous," said Helen with a grin. "If you know what I mean."

Stevie realized that the Broadway show and going backstage and eating at a restaurant had been fun, but not incredible. She hadn't missed out on as much as she'd thought. Actually, she'd had a good time at the hotel with Ms. Dodge.

As everyone was leaving, Stevie went over to Ms. Dodge and hugged her. "I liked our time together," she said.

Ms. Dodge looked startled, and then touched. "Thanks, Stevie. That really means a lot." She hugged Stevie back.

CAROLE WAS IN front of a huge audience. They were pointing at her and laughing. When she looked around, trying to figure out why they were laughing, they laughed even harder. The sea of faces was huge and frightening. Where was she? What was going on?

There was something on her head. She reached up and touched the thing. It was smooth and conical. She ran her fingers up the sides. By this time the people in the audience were crying from laughter.

Carole touched the top and felt that it was pointed. She held the point of the thing and pulled it off. It was a dunce cap. She looked around. She was all alone on the stage. There was no one to help her.

A bell rang. The audience laughed. Carole searched for the bell. It wasn't hanging from the ceiling of the theater. It wasn't in the wings. She opened her eyes. It was the telephone. The whole thing had been a dream. She lay in bed for a second, getting used to the fact that she was at home in her room. Gradually her heart stopped pounding.

She looked at the clock next to her bed. It was after midnight.

She heard a thump on the other side of the room and turned on the light. Lisa had gotten out of her sleeping bag and was standing up, looking half-asleep.

Carole picked up the phone. "Hello?"

"Did I wake you?" came a snooty voice.

Carole would know that voice anywhere. "Yes, Veronica, you woke me," she said. "People don't usually phone after midnight."

"I guess I'm just on West Coast time," said Veronica.

"Did you move to California?" asked Carole hopefully.

"No," Veronica said. "It's my agent. He lives in L.A., naturally. And he talked and talked. I couldn't get him off the phone."

Carole rubbed her eyes. *This might be part of the nightmare.*

"I bet you're dying to know what my agency is," Veronica said.

79

"No," said Carole.

"It's FMG. Famous Management Group," Veronica said. "They handle all the top stars."

"Veronica, drink a glass of hot milk and go to sleep," said Carole.

"FMG manages Skye Ransom," Veronica said.

Carole blinked. "So?" she said.

"Someone sent FMG a tape of the 'Genius Kids' segments," Veronica said. "And they went nuts. They said I was fabulous. They say I'm a natural."

Carole looked helplessly over at Lisa.

"In two weeks Skye Ransom is going to start shooting *Full Gallop*. It's a horse movie. And I'm probably going to costar," Veronica said.

Carole had a sick feeling that Veronica might be telling the truth.

"You'll be able to see the movie—at your local theater," Veronica said. She hung up.

Lisa stood at the foot of Carole's bed with her eyes wide but vague. "What's up?" she said.

Carole knew that Lisa was really fond of Skye. It would make her sick to hear that Veronica was going to be in a movie with him. "I think you'd better sit down," she said.

Lisa sat on the end of the bed.

"That was Veronica," Carole said. "She claims she's up for a role in a Skye Ransom movie."

Lisa was suddenly awake. "What?" she said.

"Who knows if she's telling the truth?" Carole said. "You know Veronica."

"What a horrible thought," said Lisa.

"Someone sent a tape of 'Genius Kids' to Veronica's agency," said Carole. "Veronica said they loved it."

Lisa ran her hands through her hair. "We made her look good." She stared at Carole in horror. "What if we turned her into a star?"

"Stevie would die," Carole said.

"So would I," said Lisa.

"And just imagine how Skye would feel," said Carole. "He can't stand Veronica!"

"I know," said Lisa. "We have to do something."

"But what?" said Carole. "I wish Stevie were here!"

THE NEXT MORNING Stevie woke up starving. She
hopped out of bed thinking that she would have scram-
bled eggs with ham and bacon and waffles and pancakes
and toast and fried potatoes and a giant glass of orange
juice and another one of milk. And then, to top that off,
she figured she'd have a serving of French toast.

But when she got to the dining room, Ms. Dodge had
saved a place for her. "Come and sit by me," said Ms.
Dodge, patting the chair next to her.

"So what's on the menu today?" Stevie asked.

Ms. Dodge smiled happily. "I'm having oatmeal with
a dish of stewed fruit on the side. I think you'll find that
it's very good."

"For sure," Stevie said.

The oatmeal was gummy and made Stevie think of glue. The stewed fruit was too sweet and too sour at the same time.

"There's nothing like oatmeal and stewed fruit to get your day off to a great start," Ms. Dodge said cheerfully.

"You're telling me," said Stevie.

The waitress came over and said, "It's so nice to see a young person eating a sensible breakfast. My daughter won't eat anything but sugared cereal."

"Poor you," said Ms. Dodge. "Stevie likes to start the day with a well-balanced meal."

"That's me," said Stevie.

"You're an angel," said the waitress.

One of Stevie's classmates choked.

After breakfast Mrs. Martin gathered the class in the lobby of the hotel. "The beautiful weather is gone," she said. "The storm that plagued Willow Creek has moved up the coast and will be passing through New York. I want you to wear your raincoats, and you might want to bring warm sweaters."

Half an hour later the class met again in the lobby. They were wearing slickers and sweaters and were toting umbrellas. They looked as if they were ready for a gale. Since it wasn't raining yet, other hotel guests smiled at them with amusement.

"Today we're going to see an exhibit on the history of

Central Park," Mrs. Martin said. "I want you to see if you can connect your object with the history of the park. I think most of you will find that you can. Some of you do not yet have an object." She looked significantly at Stevie. "This is your last chance."

Stevie resolved that she would find the best, most educational object on earth.

As they entered Central Park, the sky turned gray and heavy. Stevie shivered, remembering how cold it could get this time of year.

"Do you have an idea for your object?" Ms. Dodge asked Stevie.

"Sure," Stevie said. "I'm loaded with ideas. Choosing is the hard part."

Ms. Dodge looked at her reproachfully. "You haven't narrowed it down at all, have you?"

"No," said Stevie.

"I can't believe that there isn't anything in New York City that's caught your fancy," Ms. Dodge said.

"Yeah," Stevie said, digging her hands into the pocket of her slicker. "It's just that I don't like museums."

"You don't give them a chance," said Ms. Dodge.

Stevie knew this was true.

As the class entered the exhibit on the history of Central Park, which was at the Dairy, Stevie resolved to really look and really care. She saw pictures of the way the park looked before it was a park. It had been a swampy dump, dotted with pig farms, slaughterhouses, and shantytowns. In those days the area was famous for its terrible smell. Later it was turned into a new kind of park—not a place with flower beds and formal walks, but a place where people could ramble and roam.

The rest of the class was madly taking notes. But the words *ramble and roam* stuck in Stevie's mind. She wasn't going to ramble and roam, of course, but she felt that old itch.

Stevie came to an exhibit about the carousel. It was built in 1908. She knew that! The horses were made of basswood, which was soft and easy to carve. There was a picture of the carousel with Ralph in the center, his coat gleaming black.

Stevie thought of Ralph spending all those years in the carousel with the seasons passing and new kids coming to ride him every year. Ralph wasn't a living thing, of course, but she felt as if he were. She wanted to see Ralph one more time and say good-bye. She knew that they were very close to the carousel.

But she wasn't going to do that. It was wrong, and it was dangerous.

Ms. Dodge came over to Stevie. "You look like you're really interested in something," she said.

"It's the carousel," Stevie said.

Ms. Dodge read an exhibit label, " 'The carousel was made at the turn of the century by the Artistic Carousel

Company in Greenpoint, Brooklyn.' " She turned to Stevie. "It's amazing the horses have lasted so well."

"See that one?" said Stevie, pointing to Ralph. She wanted more than anything to tell Ms. Dodge about Ralph and what a great horse he was. But she couldn't do that. "I think he looks great," Stevie said.

"You really do love horses," Ms. Dodge said. "It's too bad you've never actually seen him. Otherwise that horse would make a perfect topic for your paper."

"For real?" said Stevie.

"He was made at the turn of the century," Ms. Dodge said. "And he seems to be of special interest to you."

"Ho boy," Stevie said. "Just my luck. There's an object that would have been perfect for me, and I never saw it."

"I'm sorry, Stevie," Ms. Dodge said. "It's too bad."

When all the note-taking was done, the class gathered near the door. Stevie spotted a postcard of the carousel and quickly bought it before Mrs. Martin headed them out the door.

"We're now going to say good-bye to New York," Mrs. Martin said. "We're going to Belvedere Castle. Does anyone know what a belvedere is?"

None of the students knew, but Ms. Dodge raised her hand.

"Ms. Dodge?" said Mrs. Martin with a nod.

"A belvedere is a pleasant place from which to look upon a scenic vista," said Ms. Dodge.

Stevie smiled at Ms. Dodge. She really knew a lot.

"From Belvedere Castle you will be able to see old New York and new New York," Mrs. Martin said. "You will be able to see the park as it was designed by Frederick Law Olmsted and Calvert Vaux. And you will be able to see the modern skyscrapers lining it."

The class crossed the street and entered the park. The sky was lower and grayer now. Three seagulls wheeled overhead.

"Birds act strange before a bad storm," Stevie said. She knew this from Max, who always told riders to keep an eye on the birds.

Mrs. Martin smiled. "Stevie is reluctant to see one last historic building. We'll have plenty of time to see Belvedere Castle before it rains, but I want everyone to zip and button up."

"I don't know—those birds look worried," Stevie said.

Mrs. Martin looked annoyed. "Stevie, we are going to stick to our schedule."

Stevie knew that weather could be unpredictable. Storms could come up faster than expected. Mrs. Martin might know a lot about antiques and English and history, but Stevie could tell that she didn't know a lot about weather.

Ms. Dodge tied a plaid silk scarf over her head. The class zipped up their raincoats and put on their hoods.

A flock of crows crossed the sky, screaming.

"I don't like crows," Ms. Dodge said. "They're kind of spooky." A gust of wind caught her scarf, pulled it loose, and sent it straight up in the air. "Oh," she said, running after it, her arms up. The class ran with her. The scarf spread out like a large plaid bird.

*It's now or never*, Stevie thought. She ducked behind a bush and ran in a low crouch. She hated to do this to Ms. Dodge and Mrs. Martin, but she really wanted to see Ralph one more time before she left, and she had a feeling that the carousel was just a few hundred yards away. She could be there and back before anyone noticed she was gone.

She trotted with her head down. She would have a short visit with Ralph and then meet her class at Belvedere Castle. She didn't know where the castle was, but she could ask.

Skaters passed her, heading out of the park. "It's about to rain," one of them called to her.

"No problem," Stevie said as the first drop smashed into her nose. She figured it was one of those spring storms that come on fast and blow themselves out. Raindrops bounced off the hood of her slicker. This was hard rain, she realized. Maybe it really was the storm that had soaked Willow Creek.

Stevie looked up. A drop pelted her on the forehead. This rain wasn't kidding around.

A parks department man in a green jumpsuit ran past her. "Get under cover!" he yelled. "It's about to begin."

Begin? So far as Stevie could see, it already had begun. She ran south, her head down, minding her steps. She noticed something very odd. The rain was bouncing. Rain did not bounce. She looked more closely. The rain was bouncing above her ankles, almost up to her knees. Something stung her nose. "Ouch!" she said. "Watch it!"

Now she was talking to rain. That was smart.

Hail the size of sourballs slammed into her forehead and hands. She ran as fast as she could while it thundered around her. There was no one else around. They seemed to be hiding.

Stevie ducked into a gazebo. There was no way she could get to the carousel and back in this mess. *Anyway,* she thought, *I already took one picture of Ralph.* She didn't want to admit to herself that she was starting to feel uneasy. She needed to get back to her classmates before this storm got even worse.

Stevie spotted a man scurrying past the gazebo, fighting to keep his umbrella intact. She dashed back out into the hail. "Which way to Belvedere Castle?" she asked him.

"You can't go there in this mess," he said.

"I have to," Stevie said. She had a vision of Ms. Dodge running with her arms up, chasing her scarf. She and Mrs. Martin didn't know anything about weather and storms. They might not have made it to the shelter of the castle. They could be in trouble. "I need to get there right away," she said to the man.

She heard clopping and splashing. She turned and a huge brown thing with a huge yellow thing on top appeared out of the hail. It was the mounted policeman, wearing a yellow poncho.

"What're you doing here?" he said.

"It's kind of a long story," said Stevie.

"No more excuses," the policeman said. "Who are you and what are you doing here? You shouldn't be out here alone."

Stevie realized this was no time for wild stories. "I'm Stevie Lake. I'm here with my class, except I got separated from them. I'm worried about them, and they may be worried about me."

The policeman nodded. "Where were they when you last saw them?"

"They were headed for Belvedere Castle from the New-York Historical Society," Stevie said.

"Right," the policeman said. "I'll put out an alert." He pulled his walkie-talkie out from under his poncho and talked into it.

"Visibility is poor in the hail," the policeman said.

"Officers will be looking for them, but they may not see them."

Stevie felt like crying. "We've got to find them as soon as possible."

The policeman thought a minute. "You seem pretty crazy about horses. Are you a good rider?"

"Pretty good," Stevie said with a quaver in her voice.

"Why don't you get on my horse with me?" he said.

"I'd love to," Stevie said.

The policeman nodded and leaned down to help Stevie up.

"Er—wait one second. What's your horse's name?" said Stevie.

"Billy," said the policeman.

Stevie went to Billy's head and said, "Do you mind if I ride you?" Billy nickered and nuzzled her.

Stevie moved back around and took the policeman's hand. She settled quickly behind him, and they set out across the park.

They went over a bridge to the edge of a huge meadow where the grass had been flattened by hail. There was no one else to be seen.

The hail fell slantways, bouncing off Stevie's nose and down Billy's mane. Stevie knew that horses hate hail, but Billy was very brave.

Stevie and the policeman rode around a lake that was splashing and bubbling with hail. They went through woods, and then Stevie saw a high building built on a rock. From up there the view would be great when it wasn't hailing. She knew this must be Belvedere Castle.

The policeman steered the horse up the rise. They came to brightly painted wooden stairs.

"You stay here," he said, dismounting and handing her the reins.

But Stevie couldn't just sit there. She had to see her class. She slid off Billy, tied the reins to the railing, and ran up the stairs.

The castle was empty.

"They never made it," Stevie said.

The policeman pulled the walkie-talkie from under his slicker and spoke into it. "We've got a school group missing somewhere in the neighborhood of Belvedere Castle." The walkie-talkie exploded with words that Stevie couldn't understand.

"No one has seen them," the policeman said.

Stevie knew she had to be calm. "Something happened on the way here," she said. She looked down on the park, trying to figure out where they might be. Directly below the castle was a winding walk with a garden planted around it.

"Let's look over there," she said.

"Let's get back on Billy," the policeman said. "We'll be able to see better from up there."

As the policeman guided the horse down the walk,

Stevie's mind filled with pictures of the horrible things that could have happened to her class. She pushed the images away.

They were following the path when Stevie saw something bright out of the corner of her eye. It was yellow and green and red, like Ms. Dodge's scarf.

"There," she said, pointing. The policeman steered Billy under a dripping tree and past bushes whose leaves had been torn off by the hail. Ms. Dodge was sitting next to a bush, and Mrs. Martin was holding her hand. The class was standing around them in a frightened circle.

"Stevie!" a classmate said. "You found us."

Stevie climbed off Billy. "Are you okay?" she said to Ms. Dodge. "I've been so worried about you." It was strange, Stevie thought. Somehow she'd known that Ms. Dodge was in trouble.

Ms. Dodge put her chin up. She was pale as a sheet, and her hair was plastered to her head from the rain, but she managed a brave smile. "I'm fine, thank you." But then she looked miserable. "It's my fault. I was chasing my scarf. I wasn't looking where I was going. I fell and twisted my ankle."

"It's not your fault," said Mrs. Martin, patting her hand.

"I'm such a fool," said Ms. Dodge.

Stevie remembered how Ms. Dodge had comforted her when she had felt like a jerk. "You are no such thing," she said, sitting on the grass next to her. "You are a wonderful person."

Spots of color came back to Ms. Dodge's cheeks. Stevie could tell that she felt a little better.

The policeman knelt next to Ms. Dodge. Gently he felt her ankle and lifted her foot.

Ms. Dodge blinked, but otherwise she gave no sign that she was in pain.

"We'll have to get this checked," the policeman said, putting her foot down. "But first we have to get you to a warm, dry place. Can you get to your feet? I'll help you."

Ms. Dodge looked up at him shyly. "I think I might be able to."

As he helped her up, she winced and turned pale again. It was obvious that she wouldn't be able to walk.

The policeman looked at her thoughtfully. "Have you ever been on a horse?"

"Me?" said Ms. Dodge. "Oh, never."

"There's always a first time," the policeman said with a grin. He turned to Stevie. "Can you bring Billy over here?"

"You bet," said Stevie. She went to get the horse. Only then did she notice that the hail had turned to rain.

When Stevie brought the horse over, the policeman turned to Ms. Dodge. "I'm going to make a stirrup with my hands. Step into it with your left foot. And then see if you can lift your injured leg over the saddle."

Ms. Dodge looked doubtfully at the horse.

"You can do it," Stevie said. "Ms. Dodge, I can tell you're a great natural rider."

"You're just saying that," said Ms. Dodge.

"No," Stevie said. "I'm sure."

Carefully Ms. Dodge put her left foot into the policeman's cupped hands.

"Put your hand on my shoulder," he said.

Shyly Ms. Dodge did so.

"Um," the policeman said to Stevie, "maybe you could give her a push."

"Absolutely," Stevie said. If someone had told her that she was going to do this, she would have thought he was crazy. She put her hands on Ms. Dodge's behind and pushed her up.

"Up you go," the policeman said.

"Oh," Ms. Dodge said. She lifted her leg and swung it over the saddle.

The class cheered. "Way to go, Ms. Dodge." Ms. Dodge smiled.

"If ever there was a photo opportunity, it's this," Stevie said. She whipped out her camera and took a picture of Ms. Dodge riding the bay horse. "We're going to put this one in the yearbook, Ms. Dodge," she said.

THE POLICEMAN LED the horse around the edge of a little pond and stopped in front of a sign that said STAGE DOOR. He knocked on the door, which was opened by a man in a green parka. "There's been an accident," the policeman said. "These people need somewhere dry to wait for help."

"You bet," said the man in the parka. Stevie figured he must be a watchman.

The policeman said to Ms. Dodge, "I want you to ease your way back into my arms and I'll lift you down."

Ms. Dodge looked worried.

"You can do it," Stevie said. "The trick is to relax."

"Relax, relax," Ms. Dodge whispered to herself.

Stevie knew that Ms. Dodge was getting more and more nervous. "How about a knock-knock joke?" she asked.

Ms. Dodge looked at her with wonder.

"It will help you relax," said Stevie.

"Ready," Ms. Dodge said with a smile.

"Knock knock," said Stevie.

"Who's there?" said Ms. Dodge.

"Beemer," said Stevie.

"Beemer who?" said Ms. Dodge.

" 'Beemer love,' " sang Stevie. " 'And with your kisses end this yearning.' "

Ms. Dodge giggled. The policeman reached up and pulled her gently from the saddle.

"That wasn't so bad," said Ms. Dodge.

The policeman turned to Stevie. "Will you tie up my horse? I'll help her inside."

"Absolutely," Stevie said cheerfully. She tied Billy to a bicycle rack. "Thanks, Billy. You were a real hero today," she told the horse, giving him a quick pat.

As Stevie walked through the door, she thought, *Here I am. Backstage at last.* She had read that there were performances of Shakespeare plays in the park during the summer. "At last, the big time," she said to herself.

She looked around and saw bare tables and old folding

chairs. There was a poster for *Hamlet* on the wall, but it had seen better days. When you got right down to it, this backstage was kind of crummy.

"Oh," said Stevie in a disappointed voice. "That's it? I thought backstage would be fancy."

The policeman grinned at her. "I know what you mean. The first time I went backstage, I was disappointed, too."

"But this is where Hamlet puts on his makeup," said Ms. Dodge. "This is where Hamlet turns into Hamlet."

The policeman turned to the watchman. "Is there any way we can get something hot for these people to drink? They're soaked."

The watchman scratched his head. Stevie guessed that he spent most of his time alone and that he was disconcerted by all these people. "I think so," he said. "Let me see." He rummaged in a corner and came up with an electric teapot. "We could heat some water," he said. "I've got some cocoa somewhere."

"That would be wonderful," Mrs. Martin said. She smiled and nodded as he filled the pot and plugged it in.

The policeman pulled his walkie-talkie from under his poncho. When he turned it on, it erupted into static. He made a face and waited for the static to stop. "I'm in the backstage area at the Delacorte Theatre. I've got six kids and two adults here. One adult needs medical attention." The walkie-talkie blasted noise at him, but he seemed to understand it. "There's an ambulance coming for you," he said to Ms. Dodge. "And a police car to take the rest of you back to your hotel. But someone will have to go along in the ambulance."

"I can't," said Mrs. Martin. "I have to stay with the students." She looked at Stevie. "Stevie, I think you should take Ms. Dodge to the hospital."

Stevie stood up straighter, her heart swelling with pride.

The watchman reappeared with a stack of cups and a box of cocoa. "Thank you," said Mrs. Martin. "Let me do the honors."

"Huh?" said the watchman.

"Let me make the cocoa," Mrs. Martin said.

"Suit yourself," said the watchman.

Mrs. Martin measured cocoa into each cup and poured hot water in. There was only enough water to make half a cup of cocoa for each person, but everyone was glad to have even that.

"I would like to propose a toast," said Ms. Dodge.

"Fine idea," said Mrs. Martin.

"I would like to toast Stevie for rescuing the class. I don't know how she did it, and I probably don't want to know, but I'm glad she did."

Stevie had to smile. "I've got to get a photo of this," she said. "No one will ever believe that a teacher toasted me unless I have evidence." She pulled her camera out of her backpack and took a shot of Ms. Dodge and then one of the policeman. And then she took one of Ms. Dodge with the policeman. And then she gave the camera to Helen to take a shot of her with Ms. Dodge and the policeman.

"Hey, wait a second," the policeman said with a grin. He put his police hat on Stevie's head.

"My parents are *really* not going to believe this," said Stevie with a laugh. She turned to Ms. Dodge. "When they see it, they'll be toasting *you*."

"You did it all yourself, Stevie," said Ms. Dodge.

"I wonder," said the policeman, pulling his mustache, "if I might have a few of those photographs. As a memory of an . . . unusual occasion."

"You bet," said Stevie. "Give me your address." The policeman gave her a formal-looking white card. His name was Michael Hill.

"I was also wondering . . ." Officer Hill paused. "Um." He looked at Ms. Dodge. Stevie could tell that he thought Ms. Dodge was wonderful and that he wanted to keep in touch with her.

"You're worried about Ms. Dodge's ankle," Stevie said. "Maybe she should write and tell you how it is."

Ms. Dodge turned pink. "Stevie!" she said.

"A very good idea," Mrs. Martin said with a smile. "I think that is something that must be done."

The policeman gave Ms. Dodge a card. Stevie

100

thought this was a strange way to start a romance, but it seemed to be working.

AN AMBULANCE CAME and the attendants put Ms. Dodge on a stretcher and loaded it into the back.

"Where do I go?" said Stevie, staring at the ambulance. There didn't seem to be any place for her.

An attendant showed her a pull-down seat next to Ms. Dodge.

The back doors were closed and the ambulance took off with a wail of its siren. Stevie thought this was pretty neat. Even if she hadn't done any of the things she'd expected to do in New York, she'd done a lot of exciting things.

"How are you feeling?" Stevie asked Ms. Dodge.

"A little tired," Ms. Dodge admitted, "and a little shaky. I'm not used to having this much excitement in my life."

"Who is?" Stevie said, taking Ms. Dodge's hand.

When they got to the hospital, the attendants rolled the stretcher out of the ambulance, snapped down its legs, then pushed it into the emergency room.

Stevie had expected the emergency room to be like the ones on television programs, with people running back and forth. Instead, Ms. Dodge was given a pile of forms to fill out and then was told to wait. She filled the forms out, handed them in, and then nothing happened.

"They're waiting for us at the hotel," Ms. Dodge said. "The van is supposed to leave any minute."

Stevie reached into her pocket and pulled out Officer Hill's card. "I have an idea," she said. She went over to the nurse who was handling the arriving patients and gave her the card. "My teacher was in an accident in Central Park, and this policeman wants to make sure that she gets good treatment." She gave the nurse the card.

The nurse's eyebrows shot up. "Why didn't you say so in the first place?" Within minutes, Ms. Dodge had been whisked away to a treatment room.

She came back a little while later with her ankle wrapped and a crutch under one arm. "It's just a sprain," she said. "We can get a cab back to the hotel and everything will be fine."

As they were riding in the cab, Ms. Dodge said, "How did you get me taken care of so fast?"

"I dropped a name," said Stevie casually.

"Whose name?" said Ms. Dodge.

"Officer Hill's, the mounted policeman who helped us in the park," Stevie said. They rode in silence for a minute. "I think it would be nice if you sent him a note to tell him that it's nothing but a sprain."

Ms. Dodge smiled. "I believe I will."

\* \* \*

By the time the class had boarded the van, everyone was exhausted. Stevie sat in a window seat, and Ms. Dodge sat next to her with her ankle stretched out into the aisle.

"What a trip," Ms. Dodge sighed.

"There's only one problem," Stevie said gloomily. "I'm going to get an F. I never found an object."

"It's too bad you couldn't have written your paper on that carousel horse," Ms. Dodge said. "I have the feeling that it would have been a wonderful paper."

"You know something funny?" Stevie said.

Ms. Dodge shook her head.

"When I was looking for help, I happened to pass the carousel, and I took a picture of that horse. And I bought a postcard of the carousel at the Dairy."

"That's fantastic, Stevie. I'm so glad," said Ms. Dodge.

"But there's still a problem," Stevie said. "Those are my only illustrations. I'll have to write seven pages of text." Stevie wasn't like Lisa. She didn't like writing very much.

"Hmmm," said Ms. Dodge. "I think I have an idea. You know the postcards that you bought at the Metropolitan Museum and the historical society?"

"The ones that made everyone so mad?" Stevie said.

Ms. Dodge nodded. "Those are from the same period as your carousel horse. They would show what that era was like. Also, if I were you, I'd put in something about the Muybridge photographs. He worked in the same period as well."

"I could be looking at an A," Stevie said with wonder.

"It's a possibility," said Ms. Dodge with a smile.

# 11

THE VAN DROPPED the kids off at school late on Friday night, and it was even later before Stevie was picked up by her parents. But the next morning when she woke up, she was raring to go. She hadn't called Lisa or Carole the night before. Now she could hardly wait.

She figured that calling them at seven A.M. was unfair. It was, after all, vacation.

Seven-thirty seemed a little early, too.

But 7:31 seemed just right. She called Carole first.

Carole answered the phone sounding sleepy.

"We got your storm," Stevie said.

"What?" said Carole.

Stevie explained how the storm had traveled up the

coast to New York and how it had turned to hail and how she was lucky it hadn't made small holes in her head and how she had fallen in love with a wooden horse named Ralph and how Ms. Dodge had fallen in love with a policeman with a sandy mustache.

"That's nice," Carole said, but she didn't sound very excited.

"What do you mean, 'That's *nice*'?" Stevie said. "That was the dull stuff. I haven't told you the exciting stuff yet. Like riding in an ambulance. We have to have a Saddle Club meeting right away."

There was a long pause. Finally Carole said, "Totally."

"Are you sick or something?" Stevie said.

"No," said Carole. "Lisa's here, though. Our sleep was interrupted. . . . We'll have to tell you about it later."

"Meet you at Pine Hollow at nine?" Stevie said.

"Sure," said Carole.

*What is going on?* thought Stevie.

WHEN STEVIE GOT to Pine Hollow, Red O'Malley was raking the ring with two assistant grooms.

"What's up, Red?" said Stevie.

"A waste of time, if you ask my opinion," said Red.

"How come?" asked Stevie, leaning on the fence.

"The ring will get dry when it gets dry," said Red. "There's no point rushing it."

Red was really annoyed about something. It seemed as

if everyone was in a grumpy mood. Stevie wondered why.

When she entered the stable, Stevie breathed the smell of horses and hay. "I've been away too long," she said. She went to Belle's stall and hugged her neck. "I met a horse just like you called Billy. He was a police horse," Stevie said. "And I met another horse, not as great as you, but almost. He's wood. And he can't talk. He just goes around in circles." Belle shook her head. Stevie pulled a carrot out of her pocket and fed it to Belle.

"Hi," came a voice from the other side of the stall door. It was Carole.

"Carole!" Stevie said. She scooted out of the stall and hugged her. "I'm so glad to be back. I've got a million things to tell you."

"That's good," said Carole in a flat voice.

"Tell me everything you've been doing," Stevie said. "Don't leave out a single thing."

"Er," said Carole.

Lisa was right behind Carole. Stevie threw her arms around her and said, "It's been a million years." She stood back. "I want to hear it all."

Lisa and Carole exchanged looks. The looks meant something, but Stevie couldn't tell what.

"We'd better do this in private," Carole said.

"Right," said Lisa.

"Let's find an empty stall," Carole said. "We can talk in there."

Carole and Lisa sounded so gloomy that Stevie was worried. "Did the sky fall in?" she asked when they'd found a stall.

"If only the sky *had* fallen in," Carole said. She flopped down onto the clean straw and looked at Lisa. "I guess I'd better tell her."

"I'll tell her," Lisa said.

Stevie could tell that each of them was trying to save the other one from breaking some horrible news. She put her hand on her stomach. "I'm getting nervous."

Lisa opened her mouth, put her head back, took a deep breath, and said, "It's like this." Then she stopped.

"It can't be that bad," said Stevie, trying to make a joke out of it.

Lisa and Carole didn't even smile.

"WCTV is running a special feature called 'Genius Kids,'" said Lisa. "And they've been shooting here."

"This is a problem?" said Stevie. "So they picked Carole and she's going to be famous."

"Not exactly," said Lisa. "They picked Veronica."

Stevie gasped. "Why?"

"Her father knows the man who owns the station," Lisa explained.

"Figures," Stevie said. "The rat. But what can you do?

Those things happen." She grinned. "I bet she made a total fool of herself."

"Not exactly," said Lisa.

"But she always does," Stevie said.

"Not this time," Carole said. "Lisa and I covered for her and made her look good."

"You made *Veronica* look good?" Stevie said.

"We had to for Pine Hollow," Lisa explained. "We didn't want Max to look bad."

Stevie thought about it. "That makes sense. It must have been tough. But I bet Max was proud of you. I'm proud of you, too."

"That's not what's bothering us," said Carole.

"We made Veronica look so good that someone sent a tape of 'Genius Kids' to a fancy Hollywood talent agency," Lisa said. "Take a deep breath."

Stevie took a deep breath.

"Skye Ransom is going to make another horse movie," Carole said.

"I know that," Stevie said. "I heard it in New York."

"And Veronica may be in it," said Lisa.

"No way," Stevie said.

"There's going to be a talent scout at the Spring Tune-Up," Lisa said.

Stevie got a devilish look. "So then we make Veronica look like an idiot. That shouldn't be hard." But then she thought of Ms. Dodge and all the things she'd learned on the trip. "No," she said. "We're going to help Veronica do her best."

"What?" said Lisa. "Is this Stevie Lake I'm talking to?"

"I learned a lot on my trip to New York. I realized that I need to be more generous," Stevie said.

Lisa and Carole exchanged worried looks. This wasn't the Stevie they knew and loved.

"Are you sure you're okay?" Lisa said.

"I'm the best I've ever been in my life," Stevie said.

Carole thought about it for a minute and then sighed. "You're right. If we make Veronica look bad, then Pine Hollow will look bad."

"Absolutely," Stevie said. "And if the talent scout thinks Veronica should be in Skye's movie, then she should be in Skye's movie."

Lisa and Carole exchanged amazed looks. These were admirable sentiments, but they didn't sound much like Stevie.

"Let's go help Red rake the ring," Stevie said. She jumped up and headed outside.

Lisa and Carole followed. "That must have been some trip," Carole said.

When they got outside, Red was in an even worse mood. "Watch yourself!" he snapped at one of the assistant grooms. "You're acting like you never saw a rake before." Red was usually kind and helpful to the assistant grooms.

"We've come to help," Stevie said over the fence.

"The rakes are over there," Red said.

The girls got rakes and joined Red and the other grooms in the ring. "You better do it perfectly or Veronica will be on your case," Red said. Red and Veronica had lots of run-ins because Veronica felt she was too grand to take care of her horse. "You think she's unbearable now," he continued, "wait until she's starred in a movie."

"That's a scary thought," Carole said.

"If Veronica stars in a movie, I'm moving to Mars," Red said.

A white Mercedes pulled up outside the ring. Veronica jumped out. She was wearing a tan silk blouse, a cream-colored riding jacket, suede breeches, and mahogany riding boots. Her hair was sleek and shining, as usual. But there was something new about it.

There was a blond streak in Veronica's black hair.

"What happened to your hair?" Lisa said.

Veronica touched her hair with a superior smile. "All the stars have streaks."

A man got out of the car. He was wearing a trim blue suit and shiny black loafers, gold chains, a collarless shirt, and black sunglasses.

"I want you to meet Joe Rock," Veronica said. "He's

from FMG. That's Famous Management Group. They handle all the world's top stars."

"Yeah, yeah," said Mr. Rock. He turned to Stevie. "Get me a cup of coffee, will you, honey? I'm practically asleep."

"Absolutely," said Stevie. "Do you take cream and sugar?"

"Two sugars, no cream," said Mr. Rock. "And make sure it's boiling hot, honey. I can't take lukewarm coffee."

"Absolutely," Stevie said. She rushed off to the stable office to get the coffee.

Lisa and Carole looked at each other and laughed. This was a Stevie they'd never seen before.

"I think they brainwashed her in New York," Carole said.

"That's the only possible explanation," said Lisa.

In a few minutes, Stevie came back with the coffee. It was steaming.

"Excellent," said Mr. Rock. "Now find me somewhere to sit, kid. Joe Rock does not sit in bleachers. Not in this suit." He looked at his expensive clothes with pride.

"Sure," Stevie said, rushing off again.

Mr. Rock turned to Veronica. "This is a cute little dump you've got here."

"It's nowhere," said Veronica, patting her hair. "I can't wait to leave."

"Don't count your chickens before they hatch, babe," said Mr. Rock.

Stevie came back with a wooden chair from the stable's office. "Should I put it next to the bleachers?" she said.

"That would be good," Mr. Rock said. "Plus, get me a pillow. That chair looks hard."

Carole and Lisa hauled the chair over to the bleachers while Stevie went to get a pillow.

THE WHITE-AND-BLUE WCTV van pulled up outside the ring. Veronica looked at her watch. "They're late," she said. "They should have been here three minutes ago."

Stevie, Lisa, and Carole looked at each other. Veronica was already acting like a temperamental star—which was just a little more temperamental than her usual.

"Don't they know what my time is worth?" Veronica fumed.

Lisa and Carole glanced at Stevie. This was a natural moment for Stevie to make a crack, but she didn't say anything.

Melody climbed out of the truck. She was wearing a

blue jacket with a light blue blouse, jeans, and the same sensible brown boots she'd been wearing all week. She was followed by the cameraman.

Veronica went over to Melody. "There's a talent scout here."

"Really?" Melody said, looking surprised. "How come?"

"FMG saw my tapes from 'Genius Kids' and they're interested in me for a movie," said Veronica.

"Wow," said Melody.

"I could introduce you to him," said Veronica. "He's totally influential. That's him sitting next to the bleachers." Mr. Rock had his feet up on the rail of the ring and his face tilted up as if he were trying to get a suntan.

"I guess," Melody said doubtfully.

"They only handle top people," said Veronica. "I could put in a good word for you."

*Wow*, Lisa thought, *Veronica's acting snooty to Melody. That really takes nerve.*

"I have an agent," Melody said. "I really like her. I don't need a new one."

Veronica led Melody over to Mr. Rock and said, "Joe, this is Melody Manners. She's one of the big stars at WCTV."

"What's that?" Mr. Rock said. "Some peanut-sized TV station?" He gave Melody the once-over. "But you're cute, doll. Send me your résumé and I'll think about it."

"Thanks for asking," Melody said. Lisa could tell that she was trying to be polite.

"So let's get the show on the road," said Mr. Rock. "I got places to go. Stuff to do."

"Good idea," said Veronica. She walked over to the barn, where Max was talking to a couple of riders. "It's time to start now."

The Saddle Club looked at each other with wonder. No one ever told Max what to do.

"Okay," Max said mildly.

Lisa, Carole, and Stevie gaped.

"Here's my music," said Veronica as she handed Max a CD.

"Your music?" Max said.

"I want you to play it as I ride into the ring," said Veronica. "It'll set the mood."

"What about the other riders?" said Max.

"They follow me," said Veronica. "By the way, I want only advanced riders in the ring with me."

Max gestured to the riders waiting outside the ring and started to speak.

"No. I want Lisa, Carole, and Stevie," Veronica interrupted.

The Saddle Club looked at each other, dumbfounded.

"Veronica wants us to cover her mistakes," Lisa said bitterly. "And she knows we will."

"Anything for Pine Hollow," Carole said grimly.

"Hey, we aim to please," Stevie said cheerfully.

The three girls walked to the barn and quickly groomed and tacked up their horses. When they were mounted on Belle, Starlight, and Prancer, they lined up behind Veronica at the stable door.

Over the public-address system came a gushy love song about a beautiful girl. Lisa and Carole looked at each other and tried not to laugh. Veronica was going all the way.

Veronica rode Danny into the ring. She touched her hat to salute the people in the bleachers. She flashed Joe Rock a big smile. Lisa, Carole, and Stevie rode into the ring after her.

Max turned off the music and picked up the microphone of the public-address system. "As I guess you all know, there has been a lot of rain," Max said. "The earth in the ring looks dry, but it isn't. Underneath the dry surface is mud. Therefore, there will be no cantering or trotting in the Spring Tune-Up. Everything will be done at a walk."

There was a groan from the people in the bleachers, who had been looking forward to fancy riding.

"You'll be surprised," Max said. "Walking can be just

117

as exciting as cantering and trotting. A proper walk takes balance, poise, and good communication between horse and rider. A good walk is a beautiful thing to behold."

"You'll see that in a minute when I give my riding demonstration of advanced riding techniques," Veronica said. "But first I want to introduce Melody Manners of WCTV." She smiled graciously. "Melody?"

Melody smiled and said, "You'll see all this on the six o'clock news."

"Melody is here to cover me as part of a feature called 'Genius Kids,' " said Veronica. She smirked. "But I suppose you know that already. What you may not know is that I am up for a role in a major motion picture. Joe Rock from Famous Management Group is here to observe me. Take a bow, Joe."

Mr. Rock just frowned and gave a curt nod. He looked bored more than anything else.

"He doesn't like being pushed around by Veronica," Lisa whispered to Carole. Carole nodded emphatically. But then she noticed that Max was glaring at them, and she realized they shouldn't be talking in the ring.

"First, I am going to demonstrate a ramener," said Veronica. She started Danny walking. "Note that Danny's head is high, but not too high," she said. "Ramener is a French word that means to narrow the angle between the head and the neck. Notice the triangle of empty space between Danny's jaw and chest. See how small it is."

Danny looked elegant and proud. His ramener was great. But this, Lisa knew, was more because of Danny's inborn style than because of Veronica's riding.

"Now Lisa, Carole, and Stevie will imitate my ramener," Veronica said.

Lisa, Stevie, and Carole urged Prancer, Belle, and Starlight into a walk. Prancer's ramener was good but not perfect, but Lisa hadn't been riding as long as the other two. Belle's ramener was good. Starlight's was perfect. His nose was down. His ears were straight up. His mouth was relaxed. He and Carole moved in perfect harmony. The people in the bleachers could see that horse and rider were doing a brilliant job. There was a round of applause.

Veronica frowned. "Very good," she said. "Now I am going to demonstrate posture." She walked Danny the length of the ring. "Note that there's a straight line from the middle of my shoulder through my hip to my heel."

When she had completed a circle, she looked back at Lisa, Stevie, and Carole and said, "Your turn."

Lisa knew Veronica was trying to make it seem as if this were a riding class and Veronica were the teacher. The thought made Lisa furious, but she knew there was nothing she could do except ride her very best.

Lisa knew something about posture. Good posture followed rules, the way Veronica's had, but it also had to be natural and relaxed. It couldn't be stiff.

*Relax*, Lisa told herself. She imagined Stevie telling a horrible knock-knock joke and the tension went out of her. Prancer could feel it and relaxed, too. There were appreciative murmurs from the crowd.

Carole rode behind her with the effortless grace of a gifted rider. "I want to be just like her," said a little girl in the crowd.

Stevie was last. There was a line from her shoulder to her hip to her heel. But most of all, there was pleasure in the way she sat and pleasure in the way Belle walked beneath her. Lisa could tell that the two of them were happy to be together again.

"I am now going to do a suppling exercise," said Veronica. "This is called a shoulder-in." This exercise was important for making a horse's body supple. Veronica rode Danny in a circle with his head turned to the inside of the circle. Danny was unusually lithe. He bent his neck and his body easily.

The crowd applauded. Veronica threw Stevie, Lisa, and Carole a challenging look.

Lisa knew that she and Prancer needed more work on the shoulder-in. "We'll do the best we can," she said to the mare. "Don't sweat it."

Prancer did the best shoulder-in she'd ever done.

Stevie turned Belle into the shoulder-in with a smile. This was something the two of them had been working on.

"Way to go," came a voice from the crowd.

When Carole turned Starlight into a shoulder-in, it was obvious that they had practiced so much that it had become second nature to them. Starlight's movements were fluid and easy. He had the grace of a gymnast. A sigh went up from the crowd.

"Walking isn't dull, is it?" said Max over the public-address system. "In a way, I'm glad it rained. We're learning a valuable lesson here."

There were lots of young riders in the crowd. Lisa knew Max wanted them to understand that fast riding and jumping weren't the only kind of excitement.

"Now I'm going to move on to something really diffi-cult," Veronica said. "A pirouette, which is a dressage move. Danny will turn in a complete circle, but one hind leg will stay in place."

The young riders in the crowd were on the edges of their seats. With a smile, Carole thought, *This is the best Spring Tune-Up ever.*

Veronica moved Danny through a piroutte, his front hooves prancing, his back hooves taking tiny steps in place. The crowd applauded.

Then Veronica looked at Joe Rock and said, "That's how it should be done."

Lisa threw a nervous look first at Carole and then at Stevie. She wasn't as experienced at dressage as they were, and pirouettes were rough.

"Do your best," she whispered to Prancer. "I know you'll be great."

Prancer's first few steps were tentative. But then the mare's front hooves began to fly while her back hooves took tiny steps in place. The crowd applauded.

Stevie grinned. A pirouette was just her style. She whispered something to Belle, and then suddenly, like a runner bursting off the block, Belle erupted into a flurry of high-kneed prances.

*That's great,* Lisa thought. *But can Belle stop when she's completed the circle?*

With one last prance, Belle stopped in the exact spot where she'd started. It was Stevie and Belle's best pirouette ever.

Carole positioned Starlight in the center of the ring. She gave him the signal to start. His hooves were light. His head was up. Carole rode him with easy grace. Starlight stopped at the exact point where he'd started and stood stock-still. It was the best pirouette Lisa had ever seen.

There was a sigh of pleasure from the crowd, and then shouts of, "You were great!" "Do it again!"

Over the public-address system, Max said, "You'd

never know this was the first event of the spring. Everyone is looking sharp."

Lisa noticed that Joe Rock had gotten out of his chair. He was staring at Carole with bright eyes. The expression on his face said, *Now that's a real rider.*

Veronica saw him, too. Her eyes flashed. "That was no big deal," she said. "Now I'll do something really difficult. A pirouette at the canter. This is something people will be talking about for years to come."

"Keep it to a walk," Max said over the public-address system.

But it was too late. Veronica had Danny cantering through the pirouette, his hooves pounding into the soft earth. His first step pierced the top layer of dry earth and sank into the muck below. Danny wobbled. His head went down. He struggled to right himself, his eyes full of fear. He whinnied and reared, and Veronica lost the reins. When the horse came down, he looked in near-panic at the fence.

Carole knew she had to act. Danny could hurt himself and Veronica if he ran wild. "Easy," she said to Starlight, because she knew that fear could pass from horse to horse.

Starlight snorted to show he wasn't afraid. Carole rode him close to Danny and grabbed the loose reins. "Easy, boy," she said to him. More important, Starlight nickered gently to the other horse. Danny drew in a shuddering breath.

Lisa noticed that Veronica had lost her seat and was about to fall. She rode over and said, "Let me help you get back in the saddle."

Veronica glared at Lisa furiously, but she let Lisa push her upright.

Carole handed Veronica her reins.

Stevie rode over and said, "And now for a victory prance around the ring."

Lisa could tell that Stevie was trying to rescue Veronica from her embarrassment.

Veronica threw Stevie a sour look, but she rode Danny to the edge of the ring. He started prancing. Stevie, Lisa, and Carole followed. As the horses pranced, the crowd stood and applauded.

Veronica headed for the gate of the ring. *Probably,* Lisa thought, *she'll be glad to get out of the limelight.*

"Wait a second," Max said. "I have something to say."

Veronica looked miserable, but she turned Danny back into the ring. Lisa, Carole, and Stevie lined up their horses next to Danny.

"What we've just seen here is a fine example of teamwork," said Max. "Veronica was in trouble, but Lisa, Carole, and Stevie helped her. When people work together, they can accomplish a lot more than they can alone. That's what Pine Hollow is all about—riders working together."

Melody appeared next to Max. "May I say something?" she asked.

Max smiled and nodded. The cameraman moved so that he could tape her.

"I learned something today," Melody said. "The whole idea of a Genius Kid is wrong. What's important is teamwork, and everyone helping everyone else."

Max was smiling broadly.

"So that's what he was after," Lisa whispered to Carole.

"You know what I'm going to do?" Melody said. "I'm going to change the name of this segment." She looked at the riders and the people in the bleachers. "I can tell that you're great together. I'm going to call this segment 'The Genius Gang.' "

The crowd went wild.

After that, intermediate and beginning riders rode. Everyone was in a great mood, so horses and ponies and riders looked good. After the last riders had finished, Max said, "Untack your horses and groom them. Then everyone is going to meet for a grand spring barbecue."

The riders cheered.

"Real food at last!" Stevie said. "I never thought I'd see it again." Her mind whirled with visions of hamburgers, hot dogs, french fries, mustard, ketchup, onion rings, and soda. "I feel a stomachache coming on," she said happily.

As they were leaving the ring, Joe Rock waved at Carole. "Hey, ditch the horse and come talk to me," he said.

"I'll hold Starlight," Stevie said. "Go ahead."

Carole slipped off Starlight and gave the reins to Stevie. She walked over to Joe Rock, who was keeping a safe distance from the horses.

"You were okay out there," Mr. Rock said. "You've got a nice touch with that horse. It's a long shot, but if you give me your résumé and some glossy eight-by-ten photographs, I'll send them on."

"I don't have a résumé," said Carole.

"So write one," said Mr. Rock.

"I don't have any photographs," she said.

"So get them taken," he said impatiently.

"I don't have time to be in a movie," Carole said. "I need to stay here and work on my riding, take care of my horse, go to school, and be with my friends."

"That's pathetic," said Mr. Rock. "Whoever heard of someone who didn't want to be in a movie?" He stomped away.

LATER THAT SAME day, The Saddle Club gathered at
TD's. Stevie had complained that after all her healthy
eating in New York, barbecue just wasn't enough. She
needed one of her special sundaes.

"I've been waiting for this," Stevie said. She turned to
the waitress. "I'll have butter crunch ice cream with pecans, walnuts, and sunflower seeds. Plus chocolate,
marshmallow, and sprinkles."

"That's it?" said the waitress, who was used to Stevie's
crazy orders.

"No," said Stevie. "I think I'll have raisins on top."

"Why not?" said the waitress. "It's your stomach."

Lisa ordered a bowl of vanilla ice cream. Carole ordered raspberry sherbet.

"You'll never guess what I ate while I was in New York," said Stevie.

"Buffalo steak?" said Carole.

"Caviar?" said Lisa.

"No," said Stevie with a grin. "I ate oatmeal and stewed fruit."

"You?" said Lisa.

Stevie nodded. "I also ate sautéed fish and broccoli."

"No wonder you've been acting strange," Carole said. "The broccoli did something to you."

"Actually," Stevie said, "I learned something."

The waitress came back with their orders. Stevie looked at her ice cream, but she didn't start eating because she had something important to say. "There's this assistant teacher at my school named Ms. Dodge."

"I never heard you mention her," said Carole.

Stevie made a rueful face. "That's because I thought she was really boring. To tell you the truth, I hardly even noticed her. She's quiet and kind of shy."

"The kind of person who fades into the background?" Lisa asked.

Stevie nodded. "Anyway, I was really bad on the trip."

"Really?" said Carole, brightening. It was always fun to hear about Stevie's escapades. "What did you do?"

"I was so bad I don't want to talk about it," Stevie said. "I even scared myself. But anyway, I was punished. And I had to spend time with Ms. Dodge. At first I thought she was the world's biggest drip. But she's really nice. We got to be friends."

Carole and Lisa exchanged worried looks. It was fine for Stevie to try to be good, but they didn't want her to overdo it.

"I actually did something that had good results," Stevie said proudly. "I helped get Ms. Dodge together with this really handsome policeman."

"What does he look like?" asked Carole.

"Sandy mustache, athletic build. He's a really good rider because he's part of the mounted police," said Stevie.

"He sounds cool," said Lisa.

"And then I'm going to tell you something that is *really* going to astound you," Stevie said.

Carole and Lisa exchanged looks. "What?" asked Carole.

"We have to write a paper about what we saw on the trip," Stevie said. "And I'm actually excited about it."

"That's great," said Lisa.

"That's fantastic," Carole said.

Now that Stevie had told them her news, it was time to dig into her ice cream. The butter crunch was even crunchier than she remembered. The pecans, walnuts, and sunflower seeds were chewy. The chocolate and marshmallow were sweet. The sprinkles were zesty. The raisins were plump.

"This is good," Stevie said. But then she noticed that Lisa and Carole were picking at their desserts. "Is something wrong?" she said.

"I don't know how to put this," Lisa said.

"We've got to say something," Carole said.

"What?" said Stevie.

"It's really good that you're going to get an A," Lisa said.

"I'm really glad you're trying to be good," said Carole.

"So?" said Stevie.

"Don't become totally good," Lisa wailed. "You wouldn't be Stevie."

"I love your tricks," Carole said. "I love your crazy ideas. We wouldn't be The Saddle Club without them."

Stevie looked at her dish of ice cream. She took a bite while she thought. "I know!" she said suddenly. "I'll be good on Sundays, Mondays, Wednesdays, and Fridays, and mischievous on Tuesdays, Thursdays, and Saturdays. Is that a great idea or what?"

"It certainly is a strange idea," said Carole.

"It could lead to lots of confusion," said Stevie happily. "You know what? I'll have to try this idea on Phil."

"Good luck, Phil," said Lisa.

"My mind is whirling with all the dreadful possibilities," said Carole.

Stevie waved for the waitress. When she came over, Stevie said, "That combination was a little bland. This time I think I'll have . . ."

# ABOUT THE AUTHOR

BONNIE BRYANT is the author of more than a hundred books about horses, including The Saddle Club series, The Saddle Club Super Editions, the Pony Tails series, and Pine Hollow, which follows the Saddle Club girls into their teens. She has also written novels and movie novelizations under her married name, B. B. Hiller.

Ms. Bryant began writing The Saddle Club in 1986. Although she had done some riding before that, she intensified her studies then and found herself learning right along with her characters Stevie, Carole, and Lisa. She claims that they are all much better riders than she is.

Ms. Bryant was born and raised in New York City. She still lives there, in Greenwich Village, with her two sons.